I0543885

Star Bright

A.M. Offenwanger

AMOVITAM PRESS

amovitam press

This is an updated edition, but the plot and characters of the story are unchanged.

100% Human-Made – No generative AI was used to create the content or cover of this book.

Note: This book uses Canadian spelling and punctuation.

Also by A.M. Offenwanger

THE SEPTIMUS SERIES
Seventh Son
Cat and Mouse
Lavender's Blue (A Septimus Short Story)
Checkmate
Star Bright

Standalones:
Martin Millerson: A Retelling of "Puss in Boots"
The Garden of Good Things

Novellas:
The Twelve Days of Christmas: A Tale of Christmastide.
With Elves.
The Forty-Dollar Christmas: A Canadian Holiday Story

Contents

CHAPTER 1

"Here, try some of this," Kaden said, rattling a small plastic pill bottle at Jamie.

"What is it?" Jamie drained the mug he was holding and plopped it on the sales counter. Coke tasted weird when you drank it from a coffee cup—or maybe it was the combination of the tequila with the dregs of the rum bottle they had dumped in that gave it that odd flavour; Jamie wasn't really sure. The tequila was all gone now too. Hallie would go berserk when she found out they'd raided her booze cupboard, never mind the stash of harder stuff Kaden had found in the back of the cash drawer at the Healing Crystals shop. They'd have to try to scrape together some cash for the Liquor Store before she got back from the Rainbow Festival so she wouldn't notice the gaps on the drinks shelf right away.

But Hallie was all right, for the most part. It was pretty decent of her to let her kid brother live with her when their parents went South every winter, and even more decent to let Jamie crash on the couch, too. She had some hokey ideas, and her shop was packed full of weird dangly bits, stones and crystals and dreamcatchers that Jamie kept bumping into with his head (that's what you got for being six foot two). But she was nice, and certainly kept an open door—Jamie was by no means the only one who'd made use of that couch of hers, and he was at least a friend of her brother's; most of the people Jamie'd seen around there were total strangers. Hallie should be more careful, at least lock up the valuables; you never knew what people would do. They might help themselves to stuff like her food and her booze; and if she kept drugs in the back of the cash drawer, man, there was no saying who'd just take them without asking! It really wasn't safe, nope.

Hallie's fluffy ginger cat, who lived in the shop, snaked his way past the overloaded cabinets and rubbed his head against Jamie's ankles. Jamie bent down and scratched him behind the ears.

"How you doin', Crookshanks?"

He liked cats. They didn't ask anything of you, just accepted you for who you were—or maybe they thought you were a complete idiot; their faces were so deadpan you never could tell. But either way, you didn't have to put on a show for them. No pressure there.

Jamie picked up another coke can and up-ended it into his mug. Nothing came out. Oh, wait, that was an empty one. He'd known that. "Hey, Kade," he said, "this is empty!" He waved the can at Kaden, then tossed it at the blue recycling bin in the corner of the shop. It missed the bin by at least a metre, but that was okay, as there wasn't any more room in the bin anyway. "Pass me another, man," he said, holding out his mug.

"There's only one left," said Kaden, pulling the last can of cola from under the counter. "But we got *this*!" He rattled the pill bottle, then he shook the pop can. "Oops!" He giggled. "Can't do two different things with my hands at the same time," he explained, "wha' I do with the one I do with thother. Other. *The* other." He shook the pill bottle again to demonstrate, and sure enough, the can in his other hand jerked up and down, too. He giggled again. Kaden was definitely hammered. Jamie knew that, because Kaden always got giggly when he was hammered.

If Jamie's mom could see them now, sucking back the rum-and-cokes, she'd go apeshit. And his dad would give him that disapproving look—the one you had to know him really well to figure out was disapproving, but Jamie always knew.

He knew his parents were disappointed in him. They'd wanted him to go to university, right after grad. Grandpa George had put aside some money for that, Dad said, but it was *only* for university, not for something like going on a trip somewhere. Or at least for trade school, although Jamie was well aware that that would be a bit too low-brow for them. Dad wanted him to do engineering or something, or even better yet, economics. Jamie had no interest whatsoever in economics. And he'd got tired of the pressure, the perpetual "What're you going to do with your life?" and "You've got to think of a career!" and, most of all, "Nobody's yet made a living playing video games!"

That last thing was actually not true; there *were* guys out there who were professional gamers. Jamie had no illusions that he'd be one of them, but neither did he have any idea of what he *could* do with his life. He liked computers, but school just didn't have any draw for him. He'd been only too glad to be done with it, finally, after twelve years of struggling. Unlike Jessica—his perfect sister had gone straight to college from high school, got a degree, and walked right into a job afterwards. And had lectured Jamie ever since, as if she was his mom and he was still a little kid in elementary school.

Jamie had stopped talking to his family some years ago; they simply didn't get him. And right after grad he'd more or less moved out. Most of his stuff was still at home, but he crashed at Kaden's or wherever when he could. The summer after grad he'd worked at one of the big orchards, sorting and packing fruit, and made pretty decent money, but over the winter there hadn't been much work around; he was running low on funds. Certainly no cash left to do anything interesting, like go travelling.

"Here, let me have that," he said, reaching for the pop can. It took him only three tries to get his hand on it—Kaden kept wobbling it around. And for some reason every time Jamie closed his hand on where he thought it was, it wasn't there. But then he got it, and pulled up the tab. A stream of coke shot out and hit him on the nose. His head snapped back and he staggered, bumping into Kaden, who lost his balance and tripped over the cat.

With a yowl, the cat shot up onto the side counter.

"Hey!" Jamie said, "watch out for Crookshanks, man!" He put down the coke can, cupped both hands around the cat's chest, and rubbed his fingers in the thick ruff around the animal's neck.

"He's not called Crook—Crook-whatever," Kaden said. "That's the cat from Harry Potter. He's called, uh—"

"He looks like Crookshanks to me," Jamie said, "so I call him Crookshanks. And he doesn't mind, right, Crookshanks?"

The cat purred, and he leaned into Jamie's hand so hard he pushed it right into a stack of display boxes, toppling them over.

One of them fell on its side, the lid popping off. A couple of blue stones rolled out onto the counter. Yes, two—there were definitely two. Jamie only had to make a *little* bit of an effort to focus his eyes to see that there were two, not four, or maybe even si-six. The cat batted at them with his paw. They were round and smooth, a deep blue with a white pattern like a star in the centre. "Those are cool," Jamie said, stabbing the finger of his free hand at them. "Where does Hallie get this stuff?"

"Oh, who knows," Kaden said. "Actually, I think those ones she got from Gandalf. I didn't think she still had them."

"Gandalf?"

"Yeah, you know, that old guy that was staying here—when was that, three or four years back? We were in grade nine, I think. He totally looked like Gandalf, you know?"

"Oh, yeah! Like, a long white beard and stuff." Jamie divided what was left of the coke between his mug and Kaden's tumbler.

"That's the one," Kaden said. "He was even wearing Gandalf gear, this huge hat and some tunic thing. Probably some old hippie, or he was into cosplay or something. That, probably, 'cause he talked like he was out of Shakespeare, too. Anyway, he gave those stones to Hallie for letting him stay at her place for a couple days. Dunno where he went after that. She took them to a jewellers to have them appraised, 'cause she thought they were star staffire—sar saff—*star sapphires*, that's what she thought. But they weren't. Aren't. Whatever."

"They're still pretty cool," Jamie said. He morosely stared into his mug; the coke had only filled it a third of the way. "Is there anything to top this up with?"

"Lemme see," Kaden said. He was rummaging around under the counter, and now emerged somewhat unsteadily. "Score! Check it out!" He triumphantly held up a turquoise glass bottle. "Bombay Sapphire," he read out from the label, "London Dry Gin! Infused With Imagination!"

"Huh?"

"Yeah, you know, that's their logo, 'Infused With Imagination'."

"Ah." Jamie nodded as if he'd known that all along. The room started to wave up and down at the edge of his vision. He tipped his head back and forth, and the effect intensified. Pretty crazy. "So, what's in that there thing?" he said, pointing his mug at the little pill bottle sitting beside the cash register.

"Oh, yeah, that," Kaden said, "'s just some pills. I think those things can give you a pretty wild trip; Hallie wouldn't let me try them last time she had some." He popped the top off the pill container and shook two bright red tablets out onto his hand. "So, you up for this?" He tantalizingly waved his palm under Jamie's nose.

"Not without something to wash it down," said Jamie. He twisted the cap off the gin bottle, splashed a generous portion into his mug, and some into Kaden's tumbler. Only a bit of it spilled on the counter. Not much at all. Probably no more than half a cup.

"You take the red pill," Kaden intoned, "you stay in Wonderland..."

Jamie grabbed one of the pills from Kaden's hand and stuck it into his mouth. "C'mon, you too!" he said around the tablet on his tongue.

Kaden followed suit, then raised his glass.

"...and I'll show you how deep the rabbit hole goes!" they chanted in unison, clinking their cups together. They dumped the drinks down their throats, stared at each other for a moment and then burst into giggles.

"But what if I wanted the blue pill?" Jamie said. His head was spinning a bit—was that from the pill?

"S-sorry," Kaden said, "n-no can do. You c-c-could try the s-st-stones, they're b-bl-blue." His eyes rolled back in his head, and he crashed to the floor behind the counter.

Jamie tried to lean over the counter to check if Kaden was okay, but then thought better of it. Too much spinning.

The cat, from his perch on the side counter, gave Jamie an inscrutable look, then reached out his paw and gently tapped the two blue stones, making them roll in Jamie's direction.

Jamie looked at them. They seemed to give off a pulsing light. Blink, blink, blink… Kaden might have a point.

"But they're stones, Crookshanks," Jamie said, "not pills! You can't swallow stones, nope, no siree." He put down his empty mug and picked up the stones, one in each hand. He held them in front of his eyes—yes, he could still keep them in focus, yup, uh-huh—then held them out to the cat. "If you can't *take* the stones, like, eat them," he said, "what *can* you do to make them give you a trip? Hey, maybe licking them works." Jamie tried it. Nah, that didn't do anything. "Or maybe, maybe they're magic, and you have to say a spell to make them work? Might be worth a shot." The cat blinked, and Jamie made a face. "Yeah, you're right—I don't actually know any spells." He stared at the stones whose white stars were twinkling at him from their shiny blue depths. And then he had an idea.

"Star light, star bright," he chanted,

"First star I see tonight,

"I wish I may, I wish I might

"Have the wish I wish tonight!"

He giggled. Wishing. You had to make a wish. So he did, and then he moved the two stones in his fingers towards each other. Closer, closer, closer—and they touched.

Everything around Jamie started to swirl—a giant counterclockwise dance of blue light and colour whirled around him. He lost track of which way he was facing, of left and right and up and down, and then he no longer knew where he was at all.

CHAPTER 2

C ATRIONA COVERED HER EARS with her hands. *Bang!* She knew that building an extension on their house would make a lot of noise, but she hadn't expected the racket to be quite this bad. And this was only the very beginning stages; the workmen had just started that morning. *Bang!* What *were* they doing? She stepped around her two youngest sons, five-year-old Dyllie and two-and-a-half-year-old Yaya, who were enacting a complicated manoeuvre of toy horses and wooden block wagons on the kitchen floor, and went out into the yard.

"Ah, Catriona Bookwoman!" called the burly man who was kneeling on the roof of the side part of the cottage that made up their bedroom. "I meant to say: you'll want to take your beds out of there before the rubble drops down into the sheets; your little ones won't like having wood splinters in their blankets!" He hit a mallet against the handle of some chisel-like tool, lifting the first few of the wooden roof shingles.

"Thanks, Fionn," Cat called back, "I've already done that. I just hope it won't rain in the next few days!"

"It'll be all right," he said (*bang!*). "We've got sheets of sailcloth we can put over top to keep you dry once we have the shingles and rafters off." He pointed the handle of the mallet at a cart that was parked beside the house, loaded with a clutter of tools and a stack of folded canvas sheets. Then he swung his mallet again. *Bang!*

Cat stuck her head into the pottery workshop on the other side of the yard. "Guy? Are you coming into the house for breakfast?"

Her husband raised his head from the plate he was trimming on the wheel and swiped a strand of red hair back from his forehead. "Can you put some aside for me? I want to get these done; I've got another large order to fill that I have to get started on as soon as possible. Or—Cat, could you bring me a bowl of porridge? That way I won't have to stop to come over to the house."

"Who said there's porridge?" Cat said with a smile. "A crust of bread is all you get if you don't come into the house for meals."

He wrinkled his nose at her. "You always make porridge," he said, "and I'd be eternally grateful if I didn't have to interrupt my work. Please, best of wives?"

"Oh, fine, if you're going to beg and flatter," Cat said, "I suppose I can send one of the kids over with it this once. But don't let it go cold again before you eat it!"

He had already turned back to the wheel, lifted the completed plate off the wheelhead and reached for the next to put in place for turning.

Cat let herself out of the workshop, and she allowed herself a little sigh and a shake of the head as she crossed the yard to get back to the cottage. Guy had been at work since dawn; it was becoming a pattern that he barely made it into the house for his meals before he went back to the shop to keep working. Now that it was April, at least he didn't have to do his job in the evening by lamplight any more, but it also meant that he got up even earlier to make use of the early morning light. He was trying to get as much work done as possible for the summer solstice market and the increased trading season that would kick off soon, now that travel through the mountains was easier again. In addition, he was working on the regular orders the townsfolk placed with him—the people of Ruph seemed to break a lot of dishes, they had to replace them so often.

Cat was glad for the income; they needed it. Five children went through an astonishing amount of food and clothing, and the renovations to the house would be eating up a large chunk of coin. But she wished Guy didn't have to do all the work on his own. Cory acted like a sort of junior apprentice to him, but he was only eight, and while Guy was very pleased with his son's aptitude for the craft, the boy could not be anywhere near the amount of help that a grown apprentice would be. And for some reason, in the last two years since Andy had left Ruph to pursue his mastership there had not been a single young person in town of the right age or ability to start in the potter's craft.

The door of the cottage opened, and Bina stepped out into the yard, balancing a brimming bowl of steaming porridge in her hands. "Careful with Papa's milk now; don't spill it!" she said over her shoulder to Dyllie, who was following with a small pitcher and a mug. Little Yaya brought up the rear, bearing a carved wooden spoon like a ceremonial sword in his pudgy hand.

Cat smiled at the picture they made with their three red-gold heads blazing in the morning sunlight that fell through the trees. "So you already knew that Papa wants his breakfast in the workshop, did you?"

"Yes, it felt like he was feeling a bit rushed," said Bina, "so I thought we might as well bring him his food, else he just won't eat again."

Yaya proudly poked the spoon into the air. "Wook, Mumma, I cawwy poon—" He tripped over a root, pitched forward, and crashed into Dyllie, sending him stumbling. The milk pitcher and mug went flying across the yard, the milk shooting out in a shining white arc that incongruously sparkled in the sunshine like a string of pearls. With a crash, the mug hit the doorstep and broke in half.

"Mummaaaa!" Yaya wailed.

Dyllie scrabbled around and started smacking him. "You made me spill, you—you—you *doofus*!"

Yaya fought back, wailing even louder, while Bina scolded them both to be quiet, trying to hold the bowl out of reach of their flailing arms and legs.

Cat suppressed a sigh and scooped up the little one. "Hush, the lot of you!" she said loudly over the noise. "It's just spilled milk. Dyllie, take the jug back into the house—looks like it didn't break—and get some more milk. Bina, get that porridge to Papa." She pulled a handkerchief out of her skirt pocket, wiped Yaya's nose and stood him back on his feet. "And you take Papa his spoon,

12

he'll need it." She picked up the broken pieces of the mug and opened the workshop door for the kids.

"Here's your breakfast, Papa," said Bina as she crossed the threshold. "Cory says he'll be over as soon as he's done his. You've got to stop what you're doing at least long enough to eat, Papa."

Guy braked the flywheel with his foot and smiled at his daughter, accentuating the wrinkles that had formed at the corners of his eyes in the last year. "Yes, mistress," he said, sliding off the wheel bench, "whatever you say, mistress!" He hooked the stool by the table with his foot, pulled it out, and sat down. "What was that commotion out there just now?"

"Oh, nothing out of the ordinary," Cat said. "We had a bit of a mishap, which led to the demise of the last of these green mugs." She weighed the broken pieces in her hand, then chucked them into the crackpot bin with Guy's other discards. "Too bad; I liked that glaze."

"Papa poon!" Yaya said, thrusting the spoon at his father.

"Thanks, munchkin," Guy said. "Now you let me eat my breakfast, and you get back to yours, all right?"

Cat turned to herd the children back across the yard, then she remembered something.

"Oh, Guy, didn't you say you were going to place an order for materials from Ilim in the next few days?"

"Yes, I need some more copper for glazes. Why?"

"If you send down an order, I might put in for something, too. Do you think your sister could go to one of the larger bookshops for me? Coshy the Poet is supposed to have a new volume of verse out this spring; the library needs a copy."

"Sure, Yeryl could do that. Or if she can't, I'm sure Mother won't mind doing it. Just write a note; I'll take it into town later today. Didn't you just get one of those poetry books recently?" Guy scooped another spoonful of his breakfast. "'Your eyes, twin pools of deepest brown...'" he recited, the heartfelt tone slightly muffled by his mouthful of porridge.

Cat rolled her eyes. "That was a year ago I got that book!" she said. "And at least swallow your oatmeal first if you're going to misquote poetry. The eyes are supposed to be 'deepest blue', not brown."

"But yours aren't," he said, licking the last of the porridge off his spoon, "so how can I say they are? Then again, maybe I just don't understand poetry." He stood and turned back to the pottery wheel.

Cat picked up the empty dishes. "No," she said softly to his back, "maybe you don't."

CHAPTER 3

*D*EAR *ANDY*,

I miss you a lot. Mum is writing a note to Aunt Yeryl in Ilim, and Papa is putting in an order for some glaze stuff, so there is going to be some mail going down the mountains soon. That's why I'm writing you again, even though I only wrote you the week before last.

Remember how I told in my last letter about the baby I helped Aunt with, the one with the really bad cough that didn't get better? Right after I sent off that letter, I thought of what we needed to do: we had to boil <u>onions</u> in with the horehound and honey medicine, and give that to the baby every hour. I told Aunt, and she said she never thought to put onion in, and we could try it, and so we did and the baby got better. Mum says she heard of using onion and honey for a cough syrup before, she probably read it in a book back in Outland. She says that different people have different ideas about what to do for sick people, like her grandmother always made her chicken soup when she was sick, and it made her feel better, and everyone in Outland does that, but Aunt never heard about doing that either.

Me and Aunt don't think chicken soup has any healing power, but we think that it's the hot liquid and the salt and probably the garlic if you put any in that makes you better. Or maybe it's what Mum calls the ~~plu plaz~~ placebo effect (I had to ask her how to spell that). It means that you can get better from a medicine just because you think you should, and it works even if what you're taking isn't medicine at all so long as you believe it is. When I told Aunt about that, she laughed and said, trust Catriona to have a fancy word for it.

She told me not to tell anyone, but I think I can tell you because you're way away in Rhanathon, that she gives that kind of medicine to people all the time. Like around Winter Solstice, my cousin Kimira, you know, Liss's sister (I guess that makes her your brother's-wife-sister) thought she wanted something to make that wart under her ear go away so Kaltas Builderson would pay attention to her. So Aunt gave her some marigold cream, which works great on other skin rashes, but not really on warts, but Kim didn't know that. So she kept putting it on and because she thought it would help, it did, and because she thinks she is prettier without the wart (she isn't, nobody ever noticed it anyway, it was tiny and hidden under her hair) she smiled more, and Kaltas noticed her, and they've been stepping out together since half-winter day.

Liss and Ben are doing well, too, and Liss isn't throwing up any more. Liss and Ben and me all think they're going to have a boy, and Ben carved a little horse on wheels the other day for his first toy. Are you looking forward to being an uncle?

Aunt Nicky got a new goat, it keeps getting out. She says it's good practise for Ben for when the baby starts to walk.

If you see Rhitha and Grandmother Urnhild at Cousin Ytahu's marriage celebration, tell them we've got their dancers safe. They were on our mantelpiece at first, but now that the workmen are in the house and make everything rattle we thought the ~~sculpth~~ sculptures would be safer in their box in the storage chest.

I have to stop now because I'm running out of paper, and Mum says Papa wants to get going to town with these letters. Papa says to tell you that the streaky glaze worked a treat and if you and Master Ekinoru want to send some ideas for what to use it on, he'll try to make some samples as soon as he can. He also says to tell you to stop fooling around with fancy wares in the big city and get your rear end back here and do some real work for a change, but he doesn't mean it, because he is feeling really proud of what you do and is always bragging about you to everyone.

Lots of love, Bina

CHAPTER 4

J AMIE'S BUTT HIT THE ground with a thud. His hand flew out behind him, trying to break his fall, and his palm smashed down on some sharp-edged stuff the ground was covered with. Damn!

The swirling blue light around him slowed down, thinned out and dissipated, and the little light spots in Jamie's field of vision stopped making circles on the backs of his eyeballs as his eyes quit rolling.

He slowly looked around. There were walls of rock around three sides of him, shining sort of greyish-blue in the dim light. Jamie giggled. This was some hallucination he was having! That big rock over on the side there, that was probably the sales counter that Kaden was passed out behind.

Jamie levered himself to his feet to go look—damn! That was some frickin' sharp stuff on the ground! What the hell was it? Rocks? But no, it couldn't be rocks—not in the shop, could it? So what *were* those things—some junk spilled on the floor? He bent down and tried to peer at whatever it was that had jabbed into his palm.

It sure looked like rocks—greyish-blueish pointy stones. And there was that spinning sensation again—Jamie had to keep himself from reeling. Bending over didn't seem to be such a good idea. Didn't want to wipe out again, nope.

But hey, what was that? That wasn't a sharp pointy rock, that was—oh, yeah! His star thingie—whatchamacallit—rock, that was it! There it was on the ground. He must have dropped it when he landed on his butt. He bent over very slowly and carefully and picked up the stone. But—wait a sec—there had been two of those things! Jamie distinctly remembered it. Yup, two. One in each hand. He looked around, waited a second until the spinning was less spinney, then looked again. Ah, there it was, his other star stock—rone—stone, *stone*, that was it. He had them both again. Sweet.

He tapped the two stones together with a little clicking noise. Click—click click... Such a cool blue. And they had given him his wish. That's because he hadn't said the wish out loud, that's why. If you wished on a star and said the wish out loud, it didn't come true. His sister'd told him that when he was little. And even though his sister was annoying and pushy, Jamie figured she'd been right on this one. 'Cause, looking around himself, it sure seemed to have worked. Even if the star was just inside a rock.

Rock. Oh yeah, there was that big rock over there which was really only the sales counter in Hallie's store, and he was going to go over there and check if Kaden was okay. He shoved the star stones into his jeans pocket—didn't want to lose them again—and made his way over to that big rock, which was surprisingly far away from where he'd fallen on his ass. He didn't think he'd been that far away from the counter. But then, now that he looked at it, this couldn't be the counter, because Kade wasn't behind it. There was just some more rocks there. Weird. Jamie scratched the top of his head, then shoved his hands into his back pockets. Dammit! His butt hurt from where he'd landed on that rocky ground.

So, okay. If he couldn't see Kaden, maybe this trip was just a bit harder than he had expected. But hey, that was fine by Jamie. Because that's exactly what he'd wanted—a trip. Dad wasn't giving him Grandpa George's money to go someplace, so he'd found his own way to go tripping. Yup. Might as well enjoy it while it lasted.

Jamie looked around, trying to figure out this amazing hallucination. It looked like he was actually in some kind of—thingie—place where they got rocks from—started with q. Quark—no, that had something to do with physics. Quagmire. Quandary. Quarry, that's what it was—he was in a quarry. There were walls of rock around him, rising quite high—well, high-ish—against the sky, which was getting dark—ish—above them. He turned around all the way, and behind him he saw that the quarry opened up into a wide plain. Some distance away, towards the horizon, there was an assortment of twinkling lights—probably a town. Cool—a town? He'd go explore, that's what he'd do.

It seemed like a long time later when he got to the edge of the town. There was still enough light to realize he wasn't seeing a regular modern town—well, imagining it, anyway. This place was like the towns in his favourite computer games, like it had come straight from the Middle Ages. Steeply gabled roofs, walls with those dark beams and white plaster in between, roads paved with cobblestones. Sweet.

It was amazing that his imagination could come up with something that felt this real, even with the help of the drugs. He sure *felt* like he had actually walked for an hour or something, and he was seriously thirsty. Maybe there was water somewhere in this imaginary town? He'd come up with the place; his imagination should be able to produce a water fountain to go in it. The ones in his games always had one.

He'd got close enough to the houses now to spot a gate, a wide open archway that was pointed at the top, leading down a street between two of the buildings. Jamie pointed his character at the opening—no, he wasn't in a computer game. This was him, himself, doing the walking, not a CG character he was directing with his mouse and arrow keys. His feet, that's what he was pointing at the gate. It was getting a little hard to move them, but he could still pull it off. One foot in front of the other, that's what he was doing.

There were soft yellow lights burning in some of the windows of the houses that were closing in the sides of the street, and he could hear laughter coming from behind the shutters. Then it got all quiet again. Jamie jumped when a small cat ran across the street in front of him, and he had to catch himself against the rough plaster wall of the house beside him. It was getting hard to stay upright; his head was really woozy. But he was so thirsty...

There! Was that running water he heard? Jamie stumbled around a corner, and there was a fountain, up against the side of a house in a large enclosed courtyard. It was a long, narrow stone trough with a spout on one end through which water trickled into the basin. Jamie staggered over, cupped his hands under the tap and gulped the cool liquid. That was better! He ran his wet hands over his face, then leaned them against the rim of the trough. Now that he wasn't dying of thirst any more, he found it nearly impossible to keep on his feet. The courtyard around him was turning in slow, lazy circles, and his eyelids felt like they had lead weights attached to them.

He saw a couple of barrels in the corner of the yard, leaving two or three feet worth of a gap to the wall behind them. That looked like a safe enough spot to sit down until his legs felt a little more steady. The barrels were just the same distance from the wall as the sales counter in Hallie's shop. The sales... counter... Maybe... maybe... it actually... was...

Somebody was running a jackhammer on Jamie's skull. Right there, on his temple beside his left eyebrow. No, the right one. Both, actually. Jamie desperately wanted them to stop. He tried to open his mouth to tell them so, but they had stuffed his mouth with cotton balls, and when he attempted to open his eyes to see who it was, it appeared that they were shining a thousand-watt spotlight in his face as well.

What horrible place had he got himself into? Why were they torturing him so? He gave a weak groan through the cotton balls, then pried his tongue off the roof of his mouth. Wait—there were no cotton balls. That was his tongue. It felt twice its usual size and dry as dust. The jackhammering let up a little, and Jamie tried once more to open his eyes. Slowly, slowly... just a tiny bit... Damn! A stabbing pain shot through his skull as the light jabbed into his eyeballs. He clapped his hands over his eyes and pressed his thumbs against his temples. Oh. No jackhammer. It probably ran inside his skull, not outside. Dammit. Which probably meant there wasn't any actual person doing this to him. So why did he feel so horrible? Oh, wait. There had been the rum-and-coke. And the tequila-and-coke. And the gin-and-coke. And—hadn't there been some pills?

He would give Kaden *such* shit for this—what *was* that crap he'd made him take? Jamie'd had hangovers before, but nothing like this—this was horrible. Torture. He seriously hoped Kaden felt as shitty as he did himself. Take the red pill—yeah, sure! What a frickin' idiot.

Jamie had got to the point where his hands were forming a little tunnel, and he could open his eyes enough to actually see something. What time was it? And *where* had he passed out last night? He vaguely remembered crawling behind the sales counter in the store—wait, this couldn't be the store, it was way too bright to be that gloomy room. But what on earth was that brown wall just a few inches in front of his face, if it wasn't the counter?

If he kept his eyes squinted shut most of the way, he was able to see a little, in spite of the stabbing pain in his head. He looked closer. The wall was made of wooden slats of some kind. It didn't go very far up, and it seemed kind of rounded towards the side. Oh, d'uh. He was looking at the side of a barrel, that's what those wooden slats were.

Jamie hauled himself upright, gripping his temples to keep his head from blowing apart, and squinted into the open space beyond the barrels. What he was seeing made no sense. None of it made any sense. He remembered being with Kaden in his sister's store, getting plastered, then having some crazy hallucinations of being inside a role playing video game—but why was he still seeing those old-fashioned medieval buildings around him?

Now that he had his eyes open more than a slit, he realized the light wasn't as horribly bright as he had thought at first; it was more like the subdued lighting of very early morning. He seemed to be in a courtyard, surrounded on three sides by buildings with those wooden beams and white walls. The fourth side was a wall with a large gate in it. And now that he looked at this, Jamie dredged up a vague memory of having come through that gate, whenever that had been—last night? Oh, yes, there was the fountain he had got his drink from. Water. He desperately needed some water. But his head hurt way too much to get up and get over there. Oh God...

Jamie closed his eyes, hoping against hope that the hallucinations would go away, and that maybe, when he opened them again, he'd find himself safely back on the couch in Kaden's sister's living room. Even on the floor in her shop would be quite okay. Please, please...

He had no idea how long he had dozed off again, but suddenly someone was shaking him by his shoulder and shouting at him.

"HEY! ARE YOU ALL RIGHT?"

Jamie peeled his eyelids apart—damn, there was that stabbing pain again! A face swam into focus, far too close to his own. He recognized the face. Sort of. No, he didn't. It just looked like—"Frodo?" Oh God, he'd landed in *The Lord of the Rings.* "Stop yelling at me."

"I'M NOT YELLING," Frodo shouted. "WHAT'S THE MATTER WITH YOU?"

"Ooowww..." Jamie pressed his hands over his ears. "Too loud... too bright... Thirsty—so thirsty..."

"All right," Frodo said in a deafeningly rasping tone that Jamie vaguely realized was a whisper, "you need water? Here, wait a moment."

His face disappeared from Jamie's field of vision. Jamie scrunched his eyes shut against the piercing light the guy's body had been blocking, and then cautiously opened them again, only a little, when a shadow fell over his face. Frodo pushed something into his hands, wet and dripping.

"SORRY, IT RAN OVER THE EDGE," he said. Jamie winced. "Sorry," repeated Frodo in that earsplitting whisper, "but here, drink it." He raised Jamie's hands with the thing in it to his face to help him, and Jamie recognized what it was: a leather water bottle. Of course, Frodo would carry one of those, wouldn't he?

Jamie managed to get the mouth of the bottle between his lips and guzzled. A whole lot of the water ran out again and down his chin, soaking his shirt. "Thanks," he croaked finally, "better." He shakily passed the bottle back to the other guy, then wiped the spilled water off his chin, rubbed his wet hands over his face and ran them through his hair with another groan. "Oh man! What time is it?"

"The sun is not even up; probably going on six o'clock." The guy's voice was starting to sound a little more normal, and if Jamie squinted, he was able to look at him without feeling like there were red-hot needles being drilled into his forehead. He couldn't be Frodo for real, Jamie realized now that he was able to see a bit better, he didn't have pointy ears. It was just his hair, a bit longish and dark and curly, and he had huge blue eyes, like that actor who played the hobbit in the movies, whatever his name was. But, no, it wasn't only that. It was—it was—his clothes, that's what it was; he had on a dark tunic and pants, and a rough cloak over top with a hood on it. There was a sort of satchel slung around his shoulder, and he was tying his water bottle back onto its strap. "What happened to you? Are you ill?"

"I'm not sure," Jamie said. "I think I might be having a bad trip still. I thought it was over—I mean, we had a few too many, and there were the pills, but it usually doesn't last that long, you know?"

"A trip? Did you just come off a travel wagon, then, too? I thought ours was the only one that got here at this crazy hour."

"No, not that kind of..." Jamie trailed off. He really had no idea what was going on. "I—actually—what is this place? Where are we? This isn't Middle Earth, is it?"

The guy gave him a frown. There, that was another Frodo thing, the guy in the movie looked worried the whole time, with exactly that kind of frown. "Middle what? Did you get on the wrong wagon?"

"Uh, no... I didn't get here by wagon at all; I just—well, got here. What's this place called?"

Frodo-guy looked around at the courtyard surrounding them. "I think it's the Blue Rabbit Inn. The carter said he'd drop me here because it was most central to everything in Ilim, so I could find my cousin's house from here. It's in Red Crow Lane."

Jamie squeezed the back of his neck and tried to rub the crick out of it. If he was still hallucinating, his hallucinations were insanely realistic; he could really have done without the pain, thanks so much.

"Ilim, eh? Never heard of it." Of course he hadn't; drug-induced illusions weren't part of the high school curriculum where he came from, not even the Grade 12 Geography class. Jamie pressed the heel of his hand into his forehead to stop the throbbing. He just wanted to lie down again and sleep it off. "I don't suppose you know someplace where I could, you know, stay for a bit?"

"Well, this is an inn, but nobody seems to be up yet." The other guy was still looking at him with that Frodo frown, eyeing him up and down. "You're not from Isachang, are you?"

Jamie, following his gaze, looked down at his clothes. He was wearing his hoodie, jeans and runners—go figure, with all this realism, he hadn't managed to hallucinate himself some appropriate clothes for the place he'd landed in. "Uh, no. Not exactly."

"So where *are* you from?"

"I don't know," Jamie said, "well, I do, but it's—damn!" He clutched his head again. "It's kind of a long—" Suddenly his stomach turned, and he heaved. "I gotta hurl!" he groaned, and just managed to turn around so it hit the cobbles instead of getting all over himself and the other guy. It was vile.

"You're not well. And did you say you have no place to go?" said the guy, after Jamie was done retching and he had given him a handkerchief he'd wet in the fountain to wipe his face, and let him use his water bottle again to get the bad taste out of his mouth.

Jamie shook his head and instantly regretted it. Ouch.

"All right," said the guy, "come on along, we'll find my cousin's house. I'm sure he won't mind letting you stay for a bit until you're better. He is supposed to help me get work; maybe he can help you too."

CHAPTER 5

T HE SECOND WAKING OF that day was a great deal
better. Jamie slowly surfaced from a dead sleep,
his arms and legs still in that state of paralysis when
you haven't quite woken up, but your brain is coming
conscious.

What a bizarre dream he'd had. Where on earth had it
come from? A medieval courtyard, and Frodo Baggins
giving him a drink from a water bottle... Weird. And
then they had sort of stumbled through the streets of
that town and Jamie had wondered why in video games
they never had your CG character tripping on the cobbles—at least twice he'd almost wiped out, hitting his
toe on some stone sticking up.

And then they found the house that Frodo said must be
his cousin's; there'd been a sign hanging over the door with
a hammer and nails on it—the cousin was an ironmon-
ger, he said—and they knocked on the door. Eventually
some red-headed woman in a nightshirt had come to the
door, and Frodo said he was a cousin, and he'd told her

his name—but wait, it hadn't been Frodo, had it? It was something else—Daar-whatever.

Jamie was amazed he could remember it all so clearly. He often had vivid dreams, but it was rare he remembered every detail of it like that. He also remembered feeling perfectly shitty in the dream. He was glad that was over; now he just had a dull ache behind his eyebrows.

He stretched, and moved his arm to rub his eyes. His elbow collided with something hard, and he came more fully awake. What the hell? There shouldn't be any hard wall beside him on Hallie's couch—only the soft sofa back on one side, and the coffee table on the other. He peeled his eyelids apart, which was more difficult than he had expected—they felt gritty, unpleasantly dry. And there was a lot of light, which his eyes also didn't seem to like. He squinted. Had he slept through half the morning? And why was the light coming from behind his head instead of the big picture window on the left where he was expecting it?

Jamie's surroundings came into focus. At the same time he realized that he was lying on a rough surface that rustled when he moved, and he was covered with a patchwork quilt, not the Mexican blanket he used at Hallie's house. That's right, the red-headed woman had taken him and Frodo to some back room or storage closet or something, and she'd given them some blankets and told them to get some more sleep because it was still so early. No, wait! That had been the dream! Jamie felt confused. Was he still asleep? He squinched his eyes shut again and pressed his palms over his eye sockets. Wake up, Jamie. Wake up! Get a grip on reality!

He slowly opened his eyes. He was still on the rustly surface under the patchwork quilt, and there was a snoring sound beside him. He turned his head in that direction, and there was Frodo, lying beside him on some straw (straw? really?), covered with the other half of the quilt. They were sleeping in the same bed? Uh, eww... But then, they weren't really in a bed. It was just the corner of some room, with roughly plastered walls and lots of wooden boxes and junk stacked up around them. There was light coming in from an opening above Jamie's head, and a chilly draft of air dropped down on them.

A plank door in the opposite side of the wall creaked open, and a small head of red hair poked through the opening. A pair of weird-coloured eyes—bright turquoise—stared at Jamie, then the door slammed shut again; and muffled through the planks Jamie heard the kid calling out: "Muuuum, one of them's awake!"

Jamie rubbed his hands over his face. This was crazy. He couldn't still be asleep—he didn't *feel* like he was asleep. But where the hell was he? And how had he got there? What was going on? He rolled to his side, and felt something hard pressing against his hip. Something in his pocket. He sat up and dug his hand in. What—oh, yeah, those blue stones! He remembered now—in fact, those stones were the last normal thing he remembered, just before things went weird. Playing around with them, and then being zapped.

Frodo—no, Jamie remembered, he wasn't Frodo, only looked like him—gave a loud gurgling snore, then stopped breathing. Jamie poked him. If what he could recall from before was right, the guy had been pretty decent to him; Jamie couldn't let him choke right there. Not-Frodo drew in a hard snuffly breath, grunted once or twice, then opened his eyes. "Whaa...?"

There was a knock at the door, immediately followed by the door opening. The red-headed woman stepped into the room. Now she was dressed in a kind of peasant outfit—a long skirt and a loose top—and had her hair pinned up on the top of her head. Apparently they were still stuck in the Middle Ages. Jamie gave up. He had no idea what was going on—dream, hallucination, time travel... Whatever. He might as well play along.

"Good morning," the woman said, "before it gets to be good afternoon. Did you sleep all right? I was wondering if you wanted some breakfast before we clear it away."

Frodo was rubbing his eyes. "Good morning, Cousin—I'm sorry..."

"Yeryl," she said. "And your name was Daarshan, wasn't it? And..." She gave a quizzical look at Jamie. "Are you a cousin, too? We only had word about one of you coming."

"No, we only met at the inn when I got off the wagon," Frodo—no, Daarshan—said and turned to look at Jamie. "Yes, what *is* your name?"

"Jamie." He rubbed his hand over his forehead. "Thanks for taking me along. And for the place to crash, Mrs, um, Yeryl."

"Well, come along then and have some food, boys." She turned to leave the room.

Daarshan stretched like a cat and rubbed his hands over his hobbit hair, dislodging some straw. "Uh, Cousin Yeryl,"—he looked a bit embarrassed—"is there a privy?"

The woman laughed. "I suppose you need one of those, don't you. Out back in the yard." She jerked her thumb at a plank door in the opposite wall, which Jamie hadn't noticed before. A privy? Oh, was that like an outhouse? That would be more than welcome at the moment. Jamie brushed straws off the sleeves of his hoodie and felt the top of his head to see if any had got caught in his hair. Apparently not—that was one of the advantages of having straight hair, it never tangled or got stuff stuck in it, even when it was as long as his was now. He needed a haircut; his bangs kept getting into his eyes.

Ten minutes later they were sitting on a bench in some kind of kitchen or hall-type place. There were white-plastered walls, a ceiling with heavy wooden beams that had bundles of herbs hanging from them, a cast-iron stove that looked like the one in Jamie's grandpa's cottage up by the lake, some wooden armchairs with cushions on them, and the long plank table at which he and Frodo-guy were sitting. They'd been given bowls of something that looked like Red River Cereal, and a white-haired old woman put a small pot of honey in front of them.

"Do you want some milk to drink with it, or would you prefer ale for breakfast?" she asked with a friendly smile. Ale? Like, beer? They sure started drinking early in the day! And Jamie didn't think Frodo was old enough to drink in the first place; he looked younger than himself, even, and he'd only recently turned nineteen.

Apparently Frodo concurred. "Milk, please, um," he said, looking at the old lady like he had a question.

Yeryl looked up from the sink in the corner where she was rinsing dishes. "Oh, I forgot. This is my mother, Suzah. You might as well call her Aunt."

"Thank you, Aunt Suzah," said Frodo—Daarshan, Jamie had to remember to call him Daarshan. He was one polite guy, in spite of the perpetual frown which he still hadn't wiped off his face.

"Yeah, thanks," he mumbled himself, as the old lady gave him a pottery cup full of milk too. He sure wasn't up for another round of booze yet; he'd about had his fill for the next decade.

A door on the other side of the room opened, and a stocky dark-haired man came in. He was wearing a sort of leather apron that had a number of tools sticking out of its pockets; Jamie recognized a couple of pairs of pliers. "Ah, the dormice are awake," the man said.

"They did travel all night, Kaltbur," Yeryl said, "go easy on them."

The man stuck out his hand. "So which one of you is Drabet's boy? Or are both of you?"

"I am," Daarshan said and shook the man's hand. "This is Jamie. I met him at the inn this morning, and he—well, here he is."

Jamie had his hand taken in a firm, if slightly damp, grasp.

"Where are you from, then? Not around here?" Kaltbur didn't even wait for an answer. "How far in the line are you?" he asked Daarshan. "You must have a passel of brothers and sisters by now. Youngest, are you?"

"Your cousin said in the letter, Kaltbur. Don't you remember?" Yeryl put in.

"Ah, I suppose so. I don't remember your mother much," Kaltbur said to Daarshan. "When she left Ruph to marry your father I was no older than you are. What are you, fourteen?"

Jamie didn't think Frodo was quite that young, although the other boy was kind of short—and he was right.

"I'm sixteen soon." The other guy's frown was even deeper than before, and he concentrated on the last of the hot cereal he was spooning out of his bowl.

"Same age as our Kelyn," said Yeryl.

"Hmph, wouldn't have thought it," Kaltbur said. "Kelyn looks older."

"She's a girl," said Yeryl, "they grow up faster."

Jamie thought it was a bit rude, the way they discussed Daarshan over his head, but he wasn't going to say anything—you never knew, maybe it was normal in this place.

"So, boy," Kaltbur began, "about finding you some work—"

He was interrupted by a kid who stuck his head through the door. "Father, there's someone in the shop wants a pound of the specialty nails, and I can't find them."

Kaltbur heaved himself to his feet, and followed the boy out the door.

Yeryl turned to Daarshan. "As my husband was about to say, he can't take you on in his shop. He's already got two of our own apprenticing; I told your mother so when I wrote to her. I suppose there isn't enough work for everyone in your town—what's it called again?"

"Arkaroth," Daarshan said, still looking at his now-empty cereal dish.

Jamie finished the last of his porridge and laid down the wooden spoon in the empty bowl.

"Had enough?" Yeryl asked, holding out her hand for the bowl. "So, how many brothers and sisters do you have, Daarshan?"

Daarshan picked up his bowl to pass it to her. "Ten," he said. Suddenly there was a sharp cracking sound from between his hands.

Jamie jumped. "Whoa! What the he-" He bit off the curse just in time—you never knew what they thought about swearing here.

The bowl in Daarshan's hand had a large crack running right down the middle. The poor guy was beet-red in the face. "I'm sorry, Cousin Yeryl," he stammered, "I'm so sorry!"

Yeryl looked at the bowl with her eyebrows raised, then shook her head. "It's hardly your fault," she said, "it must have already been partly cracked. Although I don't remember a crack in any of those bowls, and they aren't that old."

"Wasn't that one of the ones Guy sent for Winter Solstice the year before last?" the old lady put in. "His ware is usually quite strong."

"Yes, it was. Guy is my brother," Yeryl explained, "he is a potter, back in our home town in the mountains. I suppose I'll have to ask him for some more bowls—or maybe, I'll get them from the new potter by the marketplace here, he has some interesting patterns. Ten brothers and sisters, did you say? That's a lot! I have more than enough to do with our six."

"Two more than we had," said the old lady. "Two girls and seven boys."

Daarshan's head popped up at that. "You have seven sons, Aunt Suzah?"

The old lady smiled at him. "Yes, seven. And my husband was a seventh son as well, of the Septimus family, no less. Did your mother not tell you?"

Daarshan shook his head. His big blue eyes were really noticeable right then.

"The Septimus family is a rather special family in Ruph," Suzah said. "And if a seventh son is born in that family, well..."

"A seventh son of a seventh son is always special," Yeryl put in, "even from an ordinary family. I don't know if there are other towns who have a Septimus family—do you, Mother?"

"I haven't heard of any. I don't suppose you're the seventh son, Daarshan?" the old lady said with a light laugh.

Daarshan looked down at the table, his frown forming a deep groove between his eyebrows. "I'm the eighth," he said.

"So you have a brother who is seventh," said Suzah. "Wait—is your father...?"

"Yes." Daarshan's voice was low and sort of gruff.

"I think I remember him!" the old lady said. "There was a seventh son who came to Ruph, looking for a bride—oh, more than thirty years ago. But there weren't any Septimus girls of the right age, or none willing to marry him, at any rate, so he took one from another family. I'd forgotten all about that! So that was your father, was it? It's a small world. And he managed to get his seventh son of the seventh son, after all."

Daarshan didn't say anything.

"Now that I think of it," Suzah continued, "your father came to visit us, to talk to my husband. And he was very interested in Sepp, my seventh boy. He was still little at that time—could not have been more than four or five. I already had him tucked in bed, and had to get him back up so your father could meet him. But all he got to see was a cranky, sleepy little boy; I doubt that's what he was after."

"What do you think he wanted?" Yeryl asked.

"I don't know—it's been so long. But he probably wanted to see what a seventh son of a seventh son was like."

"But if his family isn't a Septimus family, it would not have mattered anyway," said Yeryl.

Jamie couldn't stand it any more. "What exactly *is* a Septimus family?"

The women looked at him. "You've never heard of us, either?" Yeryl said. "I thought everyone knew, at least in Isachang."

Jamie shook his head. For one thing, he wasn't from—whatever she'd just said, but he wasn't about to say so.

"The Septimus family is a long line of people with special powers," the old lady explained. "One of their ancestors was a seventh son of a seventh son, a long time ago—hundreds and hundreds of years—and it started with him. Probably—maybe even before then. And he passed his gifts down to his descendants. They are all gifted, in one way or another; but if there is a seventh son born in that family, he has extra abilities. My husband could make things work—if he put his hands to a task, it would always turn out right, no matter what it was. And now my son, Guy—"

Jamie was confused. He thought she'd called him Sepp a minute ago. His confusion must have shown on his face, because Yeryl laughed.

"It's complicated," she said. "Growing up, we thought Sepp was my father's seventh son—we didn't know then he'd had another son, with another woman. Sepp is actually father's eighth, and Guy—my second-youngest brother—is the seventh, the Septimissimus."

Now Daarshan's eyes looked like total saucers in his face, and Yeryl seemed to have noticed it, too.

"I suppose Sepp's just like you, then," she said to him. "The eighth son of a seventh son. Maybe you should meet him."

Then she turned to Jamie. "We have only been talking about us and our family—where do you come in? Are you from Arkaroth, as well? A cousin, or..."

Jamie cleared his throat. He had no idea how much he should tell them—for that matter, he didn't know much himself. He still had no idea what was going on, how he had ended up in this place. It all *felt* real enough, there was none of that surreal sensation that came with even the most vivid dream, where things shifted from one thing to another without explanation or sense. What these people were talking about was strange, certainly, and the surroundings were like nothing Jamie had ever seen be-fore—outside of computer games and movie screens, of course—but within that setting, it all seemed to fit togeth-er. Internal consistency, they called it in gaming. And that Red River Cereal hadn't tasted bad, either.

Daarshan helped him out.

"Jamie isn't from Arkaroth," he said. "I already said, we only met when I got off the wagon at that inn. And I think"—he gave Jamie that appraising look again—"he's not even from anywhere else in Isachang, are you?"

Jamie drew a deep breath. Well, if he was put on the spot like that… "I don't even know what Isa-Isachang is," he said. They all stared at him. Oh well. In for a penny, in for a pound. They'd probably think he was insane—and as he wasn't so sure about that himself at the moment, it hardly mattered.

"I sort of just, I guess, dropped here. Last night, outside of town, in some kind of quarry. Then I walked here. Last I remember, I was with my friend, Kaden, and we, umm, did stuff," (no call to tell them about the booze. Or the pills. They'd probably not get it anyway) "and then I was in that quarry. No idea how or why or anything, or how I can get back."

Daarshan did that saucer thing with his eyes again. But for some reason, the two women didn't look at Jamie as if they thought he was nuts. Yeryl's eyebrows had climbed halfway up her forehead, and she and her mother were looking at each other with a strange expression on their faces.

"You just dropped here?" Yeryl said. "From—from someplace that's not—well, not Isachang?"

"Yes, pretty much." It sure sounded crazy, even to himself. Jamie started to sweat a little, and he stabbed his fingers through his hair, swiping it off his forehead.

Yeryl looked at her mother. "That sounds exactly like what happened to Catriona and Nicky, doesn't it?"

CHAPTER 6

*D*EAR *A*NDY, SOMETHING HORRIBLY *sad has happened: You're not going to be an uncle after all. This
is the first time all day that I've been able to stop crying.
I knew right away when something was going wrong with
Liss's baby, I could feel it—Liss is my cousin, you know. I was
at home, it was first thing in the morning, and I hadn't gone
to Aunt's house yet, so I couldn't get there as fast as I needed
to. Aunt went over to Liss and Ben's right away, as soon as
she felt it, but there was nothing she could do. When I got
there, it was all over. Aunt wouldn't let me in the room at
first; she says I'm not ready for helping in a birthing room
yet. But afterwards, I saw her, Andy, I saw my little cousin.
It was a baby girl after all, not a boy like we all thought. She
was so tiny, no bigger than my hand, and she looked like she
was asleep, all curled up with her tiny, tiny fingers and toes.
I guess she couldn't even open her eyes yet. We wrapped her
in a soft cloth, and Liss held her in her hands and she cried
and she cried. ~~And~~*

*Dear Andy, I'm going to start over again. I stopped yes-
terday because Papa came in. Andy, that cup you sent—did*

you know? Did you know about the baby, and about what Ben was making? But you couldn't have; you sent the cup days ago, when we didn't know anything was going to be wrong with the baby. Papa didn't know what you wanted done with the cup; he said you sent a note with it telling him to give the cup to me, so that's why he brought it over to the house right away. He hadn't even tried out what you said to do, and so we did it together, we put a candle inside the cup like you said, and we lit it up. Andy, it's beautiful! It looks just like a normal pretty cup made like your other special white ware, but when there is a light inside it, it glows! Mum says it looks like something called alabaster, which is a soft stone you can carve that the light shines through just like this. Papa says he's never seen anything like it, it must be a really special clay.

And Andy—the daisy flowers you made on it, that shine so beautifully when there is a light inside, they're exactly like the ones Ben carved on the little box. But you already knew that, didn't you? You probably didn't know why you made daisies on the cup, but you had to. Because they were for the baby. Ben worked on the box all night, he made it out of holly wood, which is the whitest and smoothest wood he could find, and he put those same daisies on the lid and on the sides, like the box was woven all out of flowers. You know those daisy wreaths Rhitha and I make in the summer sometimes? Like that, except a whole box out of it. And Andy, I can tell you because you're Ben's brother, but there were water spots all over the box from where he cried when he was carving it. I think he cried the whole night.

And so this morning, we laid little Daisy to sleep in the box, wrapped in the softest piece of flannel we could find, on a little wool pillow to cushion her. That was her name, Daisy; that's why you and Ben made her those flowers on her bed and her lantern. We took her to the Garden of Peace, and we put her to rest in the Children's Corner under the big willow tree; and we planted some daisies in the spot, and then we put the cup on top with a candle lit inside it. Guthna Caretaker is going to keep the candle lit for three days and nights, and then, she said, she'll keep lighting it whenever she thinks of it. Guthna always knows where people's resting spots are, even though we don't put stones with their names over top like Mum says they do in her old world, but she liked the lantern cup; she says it's one more thing to remember Baby Daisy by.

I always liked the Garden of Peace; we played there when I was little. And now I'm going to sing a lullaby for Baby Daisy every time I go there. We sang her one when we lit the candle, but Liss was crying so much she couldn't sing. Liss is at home now, and her mother is there looking after her. I have to go soon and bring them a pot of soup and some buns Mum made; they're almost finished.

But Andy, there's one more thing that happened. I still don't know what to make of it. After we put Baby Daisy to sleep in the Garden of Peace, we took Ben and Liss home, and Aunt sent me to her house to pick up some medicine herbs. And, Andy, I didn't do what she asked me to do. Well, I did mostly, but not all of it. She said to bring sage for a brew to help Liss's milk dry up. But it wasn't right! I just know it wasn't. So I didn't bring it. Aunt was angry with me. I've never made her angry like that before. I mean, she scolds, but

I've never disobeyed her like this. She said I was too young to understand, and that the milk coming in would hurt Liss and I shouldn't let my feelings about Daisy stop me from doing what was necessary. But it wasn't that! I just know that it would be wrong to dry up Liss's milk, and not because of Daisy. I'm really sad about the baby myself, and it's even harder to feel Liss's and Ben's sadness—I wish I could stop feeling everyone's feelings all the time. But that's not why I didn't bring the sage for the brew. I tried to explain that to Aunt, and then Mum backed me up, because she knew how I was feeling, so Aunt gave in, even though she didn't like it. I only hope Liss won't hurt too much. I don't know why it would be wrong to dry up her milk, but I just know it is.

I have to go, the buns are ready. I wish you were here, Andy.

Love, Bina

CHAPTER 7

T HE CART CREAKED ALONG the forest road, hitting yet another bump, or log, or rock, or whatever it was. Jamie shifted uncomfortably on the hard bench. His tail bone would never be the same again. And they had only been on the road for three or four hours, he figured—he didn't have a watch on him, and nobody else had a timepiece either, so he had to take a guess at the time from the position of the sun.

"So how long did they say this was going to take?"

Frodo—no, Daarshan—turned to him and raised his eyebrows.

"You asked that three times already," he said. "Two days, if all goes well. Do you think it will go any faster if you keep asking?"

Jamie gave a rueful grin.

"That's what my mom used to say when we went on road trips when I was a kid." What he wouldn't give for the nice, soft, cushioned back seat of his dad's Honda right now! Not to mention the smooth asphalt of a freeway, with the wind zipping past the car window as you travelled along, and Mom's infernal country music blaring on the stereo... You didn't appreciate these things until you were stuck in a wooden cart drawn by a pair of big old horses—Clydesdales or something; his sister would know—rattling through the woods on a path that made the worst logging road at home look like a race track. And this would go on for another two frickin' *days*! "How can you stand this? It takes forever, and it's literally a pain in the butt!"

"We could get out and walk for a spell," Daarshan said, "if your shoes are up to it."

He gave a dubious glance at Jamie's running shoes, the only piece of non-local clothing Jamie still wore. Yeryl had loaned him an outfit that belonged to her eldest son, who was almost as tall as Jamie—he took after her brother, she said. This was the potter guy who'd made that dish that had broken in Daar's hands, to whose house they were headed on this infernal torture device that called itself a travelling cart. Yeryl's kid's clothes fit Jamie well enough—the pants were a bit wide in the waist, which was usually the way it was, but they had a drawstring, so it didn't matter. But for shoes, there had been nothing doing—no spare size 13 footwear kicking around the place, apparently. Jamie was thankful enough for the gear they'd let him have, anyway. They hadn't had an extra cloak like the Frodo one Daarshan was wearing, but they'd given him a blanket which supposedly he'd need in the night. Oh man—if the accommodations were as rustic as the transportation, this could be interesting.

"Yeah, let's walk," he said. "Do we just hop off?"

"Pretty much," Daarshan said. He turned to the front of the cart where the view was blocked by the wide-brimmed hat of the driver, a short middle-aged man whose name Jamie hadn't quite caught when they set out—people had weird names here, hard to remember—and tapped the man on the shoulder. "We're going to walk for a bit," he said.

"Suit yourselves," said the driver over his shoulder. "The horses won't mind having a bit less of a load. Need me to pull up so you can get out?"

Daar got up from the bench seat that was running along the inside of the cart length-wise. "No, we can manage," he said.

"Says you," said Jamie, grabbing onto the side rail of the carriage to keep from getting tossed into the lap of the other passenger by the jostling of the carriage. From the dirty look the woman gave him, landing on top of her would not be a good idea.

She wasn't all that old, Jamie figured, probably somewhere around the same age as his sister, in her mid-twenties. It was kind of hard to tell, though, because she wore a big cloak with the hood up most of the time. Her face could have been pretty if she didn't have such a sourpuss expression all the time, and when her hood had slipped back, Jamie had seen that her hair was long and straight, a shiny black. No telling about her figure, though, because of that cloak.

She hadn't introduced herself; hadn't said anything beyond the first sentence at the inn yard. "Is this the carriage to Ruph?" she'd asked, and when the driver said it was, she'd handed him a couple of coins, climbed on the cart, shoved a parcel off the left-hand bench, sat herself down, and proceeded to ignore the rest of them.

Jamie jumped off the tailgate of the cart. The vehicle, if you wanted to call it that, was only going walking speed to begin with, so keeping up shouldn't be a problem. It felt good to stretch his legs.

"So what do you think of her?" he asked Daar, once the cart had got some steps ahead of them and they weren't in earshot any more. He pointed with his chin at the woman in the carriage.

"What's there to think of?"

"She's not exactly friendly, is she?"

Daarshan shrugged.

"Some folks keep themselves to themselves," he said. "If she doesn't want to talk, that's her outlook."

"I suppose," Jamie said. "But she could crack a smile once in a while, not look at us like we crawled out from under a rock."

"Well, you did," said Daar, "or at least crawled out from behind some cider barrels." He gave Jamie a sidelong glance, the corner of his mouth twitching a bit.

"What? You—you—"

Jamie landed a punch on Daar's shoulder, but to his surprise he got a punch right back. They hit, pushed and slapped each other, until eventually Jamie got such a shove, he landed on his ass in the bushes by the side of the road, flailing his arms, a sharp twig poking into his ear. With a grin, Daar held out his hand and hauled Jamie back to his feet.

Daar packed a fairly decent punch for a guy as short as he was, and Jamie was starting to suspect that behind that perpetual Frodo frown hid a considerable sense of humour. He'd been outright baiting Jamie with that cider barrel comment. It was almost like he was used to that kind of tussle with other guys. That was right—hadn't he said he had a whole bunch of older brothers?

Jamie beat the dirt off the backside of his pants, and when he looked up, he met the eyes of the woman in the cart, looking at him with a sneer. Right away she looked the other direction, staring ahead past the driver's shoulder. What a friendly travelling companion that chick was! And there was no call for her to look like that just because he'd got his pants dirty.

"So, tell me about this Ruph place," Jamie said to Daarshan as they fell back into step behind the cart.

"I don't know anything about it," Daar said. He'd picked up a heavy piece of tree branch from the side of the road and was using it as a walking stick, making him look more than ever like Frodo Baggins on his way to Mordor.

"I thought that's where your mother is from?"

"Yes. But I've never been there, and she didn't say anything about it. At least not to me." There was that slightly bitter tone in Daar's voice again, and when Jamie turned to look at him, he saw that the Frodo frown was quite pronounced.

Suddenly there was a splintering noise, and Daar dropped his stick. "Ouch!"

Jamie stopped and picked up the branch, which had split halfway down its length.

"Wow, that's weird," he said. "There must have been some serious tension in that wood! Look, you could use it as a dowsing rod." He held the now-forked stick by its two broken ends and pointed it at the ground

"Leave it," Daarshan said curtly. "I'll find another one."

"As you wish!" Jamie said in his best *Princess Bride* voice (his mom and sister were crazy about that movie). He tossed the broken stick into the bushes, startling some small creature, which rustled away through the under-brush. "Sorry!" he called after it.

Daar gave a snort. "Who're you apologizing to?"

"That chipmunk or whatever I just hit over the head with the stick," Jamie said.

"Chip-what?"

"Chipmunk! You know, small squirrelly thing?"

Daarshan gave him a blank look, and in that moment, Jamie became sharply aware again that he was in a foreign country—a whole foreign *world*. He'd almost forgotten it—well, shoved it to the back of his consciousness. To be honest, he was still not entirely sure that the whole ex-perience wasn't some extremely elaborate and hyper-vivid dream, but after the first couple of days at Yeryl's house in—what was the town called again? Oh, Ilim—after the first couple of days in Ilim, he had pretty much told him-self that he might as well go with the flow and treat this whole deal as real. Which basically meant he'd been sucked off into this world he was in now by some weird magical process. It wasn't actually as bizarre and freaky as it might be, because according to Yeryl, that's what had happened to two of her sisters-in-law, too—the one called Cat, and the other whose name Jamie couldn't remember—they'd come from what Yeryl called 'Outland', another world, which sounded like it could well be Jamie's own home.

And that's why Jamie was on his way up into the mountains in a snail's-paced wooden cart, to talk to those sisters-in-law to see if there was maybe a way to get home again, somehow. And then, the same sisters-in-law just happened to be married to those two brothers of Yeryl's that she figured Daarshan should talk to, the potter and the other one, the seventh and eighth sons. Well, at least she said that she thought that; Jamie was wondering if they weren't just shipping Daar off because they didn't have a job for him in their shop. But he was glad to have his company on this trip; at least Daar knew what was going on, and he was a nice guy.

"So if you don't know anything about this Ruph place, what's your home town like?"

"Arkaroth? It's—well, it's a town. Smallish."

"Where is it at? Are we going anywhere near it?"

"No. We're going into the mountains. Arkaroth is by the sea."

"I see," Jamie said. "Haha, get it?"

All at once the cart in front of them bounced, there was a crunching noise and it lurched sharply to its side. The woman screamed as she was half tossed out of the vehicle.

CHAPTER 8

"**D**AMN AND BLAST IT!" the driver muttered. He was squatting beside the cart, inspecting the broken wheel. "That's just what we needed. I don't have the tools to fix this here; they got left at the waystation last time. Couldn't have held for another two hours, could it? Damn!"

The woman was sitting on a dryish log by the side of the road, scowling at the driver, the cart, the trees and bushes, and most of all Jamie and Daarshan. Heck, Jamie thought, she was probably scowling on principle. She seemed to be like that. Now that she had got out of the cart, Jamie got a better look at her. She was fat—not her face so much, but her body, around the middle. As he had noticed before, her face could have been pretty, if it hadn't been for the scowl, but her figure didn't seem to be anything to write home about.

"Blast it!" The driver was poking at the wheel axle with a knife. "Cracked right off!" He got to his feet and kicked at a triangular rock, about a foot long and shaped like a little ramp, that lay behind the wheel. "That's what's done it," he said gloomily. "Bumped over it and came down with a crack."

Jamie wandered over and looked over the small man's shoulder at the broken wheel. Not that he expected to be able to do anything. He hadn't taken any shop classes in high school—not automechanics, and not even woodworking (except for that starter class in Grade 9, where he'd made a mantelpiece clock—it still didn't have that piece of glass put in its front to protect the clock face. And now he might never get back to make sure it got done...). Then again, automechanics would be patently useless in this place, anyway.

Daarshan finished tying the reins of the horses to a tree branch. That was another thing Jamie was useless at, dealing with animals, but Daar seemed to at least know how to unhitch a team. That was probably normal for around here—like any kid back home knew how to put gas in a car and learned to drive it, sooner or later. Daar skirted around the woman with an intent look on his face and squatted down to take a look at the wheel. Then he laid flat on his back and wriggled himself under the cart.

"Hmph," his voice came, rather muffled, from underneath the vehicle. His groping hand emerged. "Pffmm ffn nfff!"

"What?" Jamie ducked his head and peered underneath the cart. "Come again?"

But the driver obviously fluently spoke mumble. He put his knife in Daarshan's outstretched hand, which disappeared under the cart. There were some scraping and

54

scratching noises, then another small crack. Daar wiggled back out from behind the wheel without the knife.

"Need a stick," he said, peering into the undergrowth. "Something like so—" he gestured with his hands, pushing his way through the bushes. "Or maybe this will do!" He took hold of a smallish tree branch and gave a sharp tug downwards, snapping it off at the trunk, then made his way back to the cart. "Got a knife?" he said to Jamie, then immediately turned away. "No, you wouldn't. Do you have another one?" he asked the driver.

"Hey, who says I don't?" said Jamie. He dug in the pocket of his loaner pants. Good thing he'd remembered to transfer his Swiss Army knife from his jeans when he got changed. "What'd you do with the other one, anyway?" He folded the larger blade out of the knife.

Daar looked at it in surprise. "Wow, a folding knife? I've never seen one of those before! It's a bit small, but—Oh, the other one? I left it stuck in the axle until I can get a wooden piece in there." He took Jamie's knife and started cutting the side twigs off his stick, then sharpened one end of it. "There, that ought to do it. Now something to..." He looked around, prised up a fist-sized flattish rock from the ground, then got back under the cart with his sticks and rock. "Oh,"—he wriggled part-way back out—"Master Kelett, you and Jamie..."

The driver apparently not only understood mumble, but linguistic shorthand, as well. "Here, lad!" He called Jamie over with a sideways jerk of his head and gripped the cart above the broken wheel.

Jamie followed suit.

"Now!" Daarshan called, and with a grunt they hoisted the heavy vehicle up a few inches. There was some banging, more scraping—Jamie thought he'd pop a vein in his forehead from the strain of holding up the cart—and the vehicle jerked in their hands as Daar banged something in place. Then he sang out "Okay!" They carefully lowered the cart onto its wheel. It stood up straight!

Daar squirmed back out from underneath.

"Well done, lad, excellently well done!" the cart driver said, straightening up from where he had been peering at the repaired axle. He clapped Daarshan on the shoulder, dislodging the leaf mould that was clinging to the back of the guy's jacket. "You obviously know carts, you do! Glad to have you along on this journey." He climbed back onto his driver's seat, and the woman got back into the cart, too.

Jamie gave Daar a sideways glance. "*Do* you know carts?" he asked. "I mean, have you done this stuff before?"

Daar shrugged. "Not really," he said.

"Then how'd you know what to do?"

"I don't know. I just knew, I guess. I mean, it was obvious—you simply had to put a piece of, of—well, on the, you know..."

Jamie snorted. "Okay, you got me convinced—you *haven't* done this before. But I still don't know how you knew how to fix it. Hey, can I have my pocket knife back?"

"Oh! Oh yes, sorry." Daarshan looked down at the knife in his hand. "Does it fold back up?"

"'Course!" Jamie folded the big blade back into its sheath. "It's got a little one, too, see? And I really like this one," he said and folded out the little pair of scissors.

"Whoa! It's got shears?"

Jamie grinned at Daar's wide-eyed look. "Yup. And a saw—here it is. And a bottle opener, and can opener, and..."

"It's a toolbox in your pocket!" Daar said, envy swinging in his voice. "And what's the outside made of? Horn?" He tapped his fingernail on the red plastic casing.

There it was again—that sudden feeling of being in a totally alien world. Jamie gritted his teeth. Well, there was nothing for it. His only hope for getting back home lay in this town in the mountains, with this Cat person they'd told him about. And the only way to get there was to keep walking. One foot in front of the other.

CHAPTER 9

THE POTATOES AT CHONYK'S market stall were getting pathetic.

"Good grief, it's spring, isn't it," Cat said, sorting through the limp knobs while Chonyk finished serving another customer. "These have definitely seen better days."

The small dark-skinned woman beside her looked around and shifted the little girl on her hip. "At least we can still get some," she said. She took the four potatoes Chonyk handed her and tucked them in the linen pouch she wore slung over her shoulder. Like her clothes, the pouch was stained with coal-black streaks, and at the sight of them Cat remembered who the woman was.

"It's Radyam, right?" she said. "You're still working your charcoal kiln out in the woods?"

The woman gave a brief nod. "Hoping to move on, though," she said. "Husband's looking for another place."

"Well, good luck, then," Cat said.

"Thanks, Catriona Bookwoman. Master Chonyk." The woman nodded a farewell and walked off, disappearing into the market crowd.

Cat turned back to the produce.

"I hate peeling shrivelly potatoes," she said. Or carrots. Or turnips. Or... any of the other vegetables they'd been eating over, and over, and over, all winter long. By April the produce was all limp and tired-looking and a pain to prepare for cooking. And the cooking itself wasn't exactly easy either—you had to light the wood stove, keep the fire going just so, make sure the pots were on the right spot on the stove top... and that was aside from all the peeling and chopping and grating and beating which could only ever be done by hand. No food processors or blenders or mixers, let alone electric stoves or microwaves. Cat had lived in Ruph for nearly ten years, and lately there had been more and more days where she just felt tired of dealing with all of this, year in and year out.

"Can't say as I blame you," Guy's cousin replied, rubbing his palm over the red-and-silver bristles along his jawline with a rustling noise. "Not much I can do about the potatoes, though; like Radyam Black says, it's lucky there's any left at all. The bins in the root cellar are getting down to the bottom. But here, did you see the fresh greens? I've got sorrel, and some baby lionstooth leaves."

"Oh, dandelion!" Cat's eyes lit up. That was another thing she had learned since coming to Ruph, to appreciate plants she had only ever thought of as weeds back home—well, back in America. She no longer thought of it as 'home'; 'home' was Ruph. At least...

Well, back in Greenward Falls, dandelion had been her landlady's arch enemy, to be hunted and eradicated whenever one of the cheerful little flowers reared its yellow head. Here in Ruph, they hunted dandelion, as well—not to poison it, but for its tender young leaves. You had to get them before the plant went to flower, or they were bitter. But picked young enough, it made for a nice salad or cooked green. "Yes, I think I'll have some of those. A fresh salad sounds lovely right about now. I've got green onions coming up in the garden, too, that'll give it a nice zip."

"Won't be too much longer before I've got some lettuces, too," Chonyk said. "The ones in the cold frames are starting to plump out nicely." He put the bundle of small green leaves into the cheesecloth bag Cat had brought for her vegetables, took her coin and gave her some change in return. "Anything else you need today?"

"Not from you, thanks," said Cat. "I'm waiting for the cart from Ilim; I asked Yeryl to get a copy of the latest Coshy poems for the library. I'm hoping she's sent it. And the cart should be getting here today, shouldn't it?"

"As far as I know, yes," Chonyk said. "As a matter of fact—look, isn't that the driver? The short fellow over there talking to Guy—Kelett, I think his name is."

"Where? Oh, by the inn! Yes, you're right, that's him. Excellent."

"Oy, Cat!" Guy called out to her as soon as she got in earshot of the two men, "step over here a minute!"

Cat greeted the cart driver. "Did you bring me a parcel from Ilim?" she asked.

The man scratched the side of his nose and grinned. "I wouldn't call 'em a parcel, myself," he said and pointed at his cart.

Cat looked. "What?"

Two teen boys stood awkwardly beside the vehicle, each clutching a blanket roll and a satchel. Like they were ordered and not picked up, as Cat's grandmother used to call it. Cat couldn't see how they had anything to do with her.

Kelett waved to the boys. The taller one—he also looked to be a bit older than the other—pushed himself away from the cart where he'd been leaning and slouched his way across to them, the shorter boy with the curly hair and the dark green cloak trailing in his wake.

"Here you are, then," the driver said to them. "It was Guy Potter you were wanting, wasn't it? Well, this is him. And here's his wife, too."

Cat gave the boys a quizzical look. She still had no idea what this was about, but she stuck out her hand to the older boy. "Catriona," she said. "And you are?"

"Jamie," he said and shook her hand, "Jamie Coleman. And that's Frodo—I mean, umm, sorry!" He blushed a bit and tossed his over-long dark bangs out of his eyes with a sideways flick of his head. "Daar-Daarshan." He looked down at the other boy, who was nearly a head shorter than him. "Do you even have a last name?"

He frowned at Jamie like he had no idea what he meant, flipped up the flap of his satchel and pulled out what looked like a letter. He held it out, wavering a bit between Cat and Guy, then made up his mind and thrust the paper at Guy. "I—we—you—you are Master Guy S-Septimus?"

Guy gave a nod and took the letter. "I am—but who's asking? Who sent you?"

The boy gestured at the letter.

Guy broke the seal, unfolded the sheet, and quickly glanced down at the bottom of the page. "Yeryl and Kaltbur!" he said, passing the letter to Cat with a light laugh. "What's this, another apprentice they couldn't cope with and are sending on to us?"

Cat looked at the two boys. Daarshan had flushed scarlet at Guy's words, and Cat could see his knuckles go white as he clutched hard at the strap of his satchel. All of a sudden there was a tearing sound, and two pairs of rolled-up linen underbreeches and a wooden comb hit the cobbled pavement with a soft thud. The boy, his face even darker than before, grabbed at his satchel, which had a large gap along one of the side seams that Cat didn't think had been there a minute earlier. He ducked to gather his belongings, but Jamie forestalled him.

"Oh man," he said, picking up Daarshan's underwear and passing it over, "you've got the worst luck with your stuff! Now your bag's ripped? That sucks, dude."

But Cat was staring at Jamie's feet, which she had only really seen when she watched him pick up the pants. Why had she not noticed this before? *He was wearing running shoes.* Western, American, *modern* running shoes—dirty white with a grey stripe down the side. Not the brown or black leather moccasin-like shoes that were normal in Ruph, or hobnailed boots like Daarshan had on his feet. *Running shoes.*

And the way he was talking...

She looked up at Jamie's face, then from him to Guy and back at the boy again, her jaw hanging slack. *What was going on here?*

Suddenly she remembered the letter in her hand, and with a gasp she whipped it up in front of her face, her eye skipping across the lines of Yeryl's cramped handwriting. *Favour... Kaltbur's cousin... don't have a place for... eighth son... talk to Sepp... other young lad...*—and there it was: *Outland*. She let her hands with the letter sink down again.

"Guy—Guy! Jamie here—Jamie is from America!"

CHAPTER 10

T HEY LOOKED LIKE THE Weasleys, Jamie thought. A whole family of redheads. Okay, not Catriona, and not the oldest boy, either—they had brown hair, sort of a Harry Potter look. But Guy and the rest of those kids, for sure. Well, Guy wasn't a Mr Weasley—more like a Bill, kind of tall and lanky with longer hair. Jamie shook his own bangs out of his eyes again. Yeryl had been right, Guy was about the same height he was himself. Not quite as skinny, though, but there weren't a lot of people who were.

The girl, there was a Ginny Weasley for sure. Ginny from the first couple of movies, anyway—she was still a kid. She and her dad had those same weird-coloured eyes that one of Yeryl's kids had, too; sort of turquoise.

Those eyes were sure noticeable, especially when she opened them really wide. She'd done that when they'd first met, on the marketplace there, in the middle of all those stalls and people and stuff. Catriona had called her over—Bina, she was called—and introduced them, him and Frodo. Actually, what she'd said to the kid was, "Why don't you shake hands with Jamie and Daarshan," which Jamie thought was kind of a weird way of introducing someone—but maybe that was normal there. So they'd shaken hands. And the kid had done that flashy thing with her eyes, like she'd felt something—but Jamie didn't think his hand had been particularly damp or cold, to make her act like she'd got an electric shock or whatever. Come to think of it, she'd done it again when she'd touched Daar's hand—that time she'd practically jumped, and her eyes got nearly as big as his. All these people with saucer eyes. If the girl didn't like touching people's hands, why'd her mother make her do it?

They'd ended up in the woods again, walking along a broad-ish forest path away from the town. The sides of the path looked like it had only recently been widened; there were some fresh cuts in the trunks of the bushes, and cartwheel prints in the raw dirt.

"That's right," Cat said when Jamie commented on it. "We're having some renovations done on the house, and the builder figured it'd be easier if they could bring a bigger cart through. Up til now, this was just a foot path; we had to carry most things in and out."

They stepped out from between the trees into a clearing. On the right stood a squarish building with white walls and wooden roof shingles; across from it on the left of the courtyard was half a bigger house in the same style. Jamie thought of it as "half a house" because the right side had no roof. A couple of guys that looked like construction workers were climbing around where the roof should have been. They had some beams laid across the tops of the walls, and it looked like they were hammering down wood planks. They were probably putting in another floor; Jamie had helped his grandpa build a loft in the cottage up by the lake the summer he was sixteen, so he recognized the technique. But what was that on the roofed part of the house?

"Uh, why is there a goat up there?" he asked Cat.

She looked up at the roof, where a patchy-coloured animal was standing near the peak and staring down at them from its weird yellow eyes.

"Oh good grief!" Cat said. "What's Nicky's goat doing on my roof? That animal is the worst escape artist I've seen!"

"Fionn!" Guy called to the builder, "how did that goat get up there?"

"Climbed the ladder!" the man called back. "We took it down once, but it got right back up, so we thought we'd leave it. It's your brother-wife's, isn't it? It must have followed us from town. We'll take it back when we knock off."

"Thanks," Guy said, "we owe you!"

"Maaah!" the goat commented.

The plank door in the roofed half of the house opened, and a short, round-faced girl came out, wiping her hands on a striped apron. She reminded Jamie of Meg, who'd been in his grad year. They'd gone to school together all the way from Grade 8 onwards, but they'd hardly ever been in the same classes. Kids with Down syndrome tended to end up in different classes, ones that were easier to handle, even though they had people to help them with the material. This girl looked quite a lot like Meg; she had similar-coloured hair—a dirty blonde—and had that same kind of smile Meg usually had on her face. She looked like she might be around the same age, too, but then, Jamie was bad at guessing people's ages.

"Oh, hi, Cousin Guy and Cousin Cat and Cousin Bina and Cousin Cory and Cousin Kell and Cousin Dyllie!" the girl said when she caught sight of them. "Mumma and I finished the bread, Cousin Cat, it's mostly done rising, and I started chopping the vegetables for the soup, and Mumma says I should get some parsley from the garden for the soup, that's what I'm doing right now, and Fionn Builder has been making a lot of noise all morning and Mumma says it's a wonder the bread didn't collapse from all the shaking and banging, but it'll be really nice when you have a new bedroom upstairs, Mumma says! Did you bring some extra pepper from the market to put in the soup? And Baby Yaya had a nap, and he played with his toys, and he's going to be happy that you're home!"

"Wahni!" came a little kid's voice from the house, and out of the open door came yet another red-headed child, this one smaller than all the rest, lugging a silver-grey cat that was almost half his own size. He caught sight of them, broke into a big smile and dumped the cat on the ground. "Mumma!!" he called and launched himself at Catriona. The cat hopped after him, limping quite badly. What had that kid done to the poor animal?

"What's the matter with the cat?" Jamie asked.

Catriona put down her basket and caught the little boy up in her arms. "Oh, nothing," she said, "he's been like that more or less from birth."

Jamie took a closer look and realized that the cat had, in fact, only three legs; his right hind leg was a little stump that waved in the air with each of his hops, and his tail drooped inelegantly sideways like he couldn't hold it up straight on the side where the leg was missing. But for all that, he looked like a sleek, healthy animal, and didn't seem bothered by having to hop around like a bunny rabbit. Jamie crouched down and held out his hand. The cat came over and rubbed himself against Jamie's knee - rub-hop, rub-hop, rub-hop. Jamie laughed, it looked so odd. "What's his name?"

"Johnny," Catriona said, "as in, Long John Silver. On account of the leg and his fur colour." She turned to the talkative girl. "Did Yaya have some lunch yet?"

"Yes, he did, Cousin Cat! Who's this you brought from town?" She gave Jamie and Daarshan a curious look from her slanted brown eyes.

"Oh, sorry," Cat said. "Lahni, this is Jamie and Daarshan. They've come from Ilim, from Cousin Yeryl's, and are going to be staying with us for a bit. This is Lahni," she said to Jamie and Daarshan, "she helps us out around here—she and her mother. We couldn't do without them."

The girl made some sort of bobbing and bowing motion that was almost a bit like a curtsy. "Hi Cousin Jamie and Cousin Daarshan," she said, her tongue that was sticking out from between her lips in no way spoiling her friendly smile.

Daar did a funny move that was kind of a bow with his leg going out to the side and back, like a dance step from some costume drama. "Pleased to meet you, Cousin Lahni," he said.

Oh, was that how you were supposed to act for introductions? Jamie ducked his head in a kind of pseudo-bow. "Uh, hi," he said, and hoped that was polite enough.

"You're not really cousins," the Ginny Weasley girl put in. "Are they, Mum? Lahni is our cousin from Papa's side, and..."

"Oh, who knows?" Cat said. "Daarshan may well be related to Lahni and Dola, for all we know. Come to think of it—how *are* you related?" She turned to Daar. "Yeryl's letter said you're Kaltbur's cousin?"

Daar had that Frodo frown on his face again. "Yes," he said, "my mother is his cousin. She—she came from this town."

"Oh, you're half Ruphian? Then it's very likely you're a relation around another corner somewhere, too," Cat said. She was herding the kids into the house. "You and half the town."

"But Jamie isn't," the Ginny girl said. "Just think, Lahni, Jamie is from Outland! From America, same as Mum and Aunt Nicky!"

"Actually..." Jamie started, then he quit again. He was Canadian, but who cared? The main thing was that he wanted to get back to his own world; a country border or two would hardly matter.

They stepped through the door into the little house, but Jamie almost backed out again. The place was seriously crowded with all those people! It was also quite warm. There was a wood stove up against one wall with an enamel tank over top, and a grey-haired woman was stirring something simmering on top of the stove.

"Look, Mumma," Lahni said to the woman, "this is Cousin Jamie and Cousin Daarshan from Outland, they've come to stay!"

It led to another round of bowing and curtsying and setting straight the record of exactly who they were and where they'd come from, and by the time they had figured out that Daar was a fifth cousin three times removed (or whatever) of Lahni and her mother Dola, Jamie found himself beside Daarshan on the bench behind the table, their packs deposited in the corner of the room and bowls of soup in front of them whose smell made Jamie's mouth water. The younger boys were jammed in on either side of them, waiting eagerly with wooden spoons poised for their mom to give them the signal to start.

The Ginny girl sat across the table from Jamie, and now she fixed her eyes on him, tipped her head sideways and gave him a straight, hard look out of those odd turquoise eyes.

"So, you want to go back to Outland, do you?" she said. "Why?"

"Bina!" her mother said.

"Sorry," the girl said, "is that a rude thing to ask? I didn't mean to be."

Jamie shrugged. "Fine by me," he said. "I just want to go home because—well, it's home. I mean, I didn't ask to be here; I just..."

"Didn't you?" Bina said, still with that disconcerting stare. "I thought you wanted to go on a trip." Was the kid clairvoyant or something?

Daar, beside Jamie, turned his head and looked at Jamie in surprise with his big blue eyes. But he didn't say anything; he just turned back to his soup.

Bang! Bang! Bang!

They all jumped as the house shook from the builders' hammer blows.

"Okay, that's it," Cat said. "If we can't even eat our lunch in peace... Dola, do we have enough soup for Fionn and his crew, too? We'll have to give them lunch in self-defence, so they stop hammering for a while. And then," she gave Jamie a stare almost as hard as that of her daughter, "we'll have to have a talk about what we're going to do with you."

CHAPTER 11

"**A**ND THEN PAPA ASKED Mumma to marry him for real this time, and she said yes, and he gave her the marriage chain, and that's why she stayed in Ruph!" Cory said. He expertly turned the lump of clay he was working. "And Uncle Sepp took the bowl and went to America and..." He looked around at what Jamie was doing. "No, not like that," he said, "you want to make it all go in one direction!"

Cat smiled across the workshop table at her oldest son. He wasn't very big for his almost nine years, but when it came to pottery, he already had an authority that boded well for his future career. At the moment he was demonstrating to Jamie and Daarshan, who had been roped in to helping Guy in the shop, how to properly wedge a piece of clay, and he was telling them family stories while he was at it.

Jamie smacked his lump of clay into his palm the way Cory was showing them, and slapped it into the little round mound they needed for the wheel work.

"Man, this is not easy!" he said. "My fingers are starting to ache!"

Daarshan looked up from his piece of clay. "Potters have strong hands," he said. "There was a story back in Arkaroth of a potter in my grandfather's time who would go hunting with the men in the autumn, and he could strangle the catch with his hands quicker and more painlessly than the other hunters could dispatch it with a blow to the neck."

Cat made a face. "That's a charming tale," she said with a slight shudder. "I don't think we'll go for that, Guy, will we?" She turned to her husband who just stepped back through the door.

"Go for what?" He put a wooden crate on the table and carefully took out some bisque ware, stacking the pieces on a shelf ready for glazing.

"Bare-handed hunting," Cat replied. She ruled a line in her black-paper-covered notebook under the calculations of the household budget, and hoped she hadn't got the figures hopelessly muddled. She had escaped with her paperwork to the workshop, as the bedroom was under construction and the kitchen was its usual hubbub of activity—Dola and Lahni were baking, the little boys had a noisy game going, and Bina was doing a herb blending project Aunt had set her to do in the course of her herb woman's apprenticeship.

"Ah, no," said Guy, lifting a stack of dishes out of his box. "I leave the killing to others; I'd rather use my hands to make pots. Daarshan, take those top pieces off, please?"

The boy sprang to do the potter's bidding, catching the first two bowls off the top of the precariously balanced stack before they toppled and fell. He seemed a very polite, helpful kid, Cat thought, but there was something in him—some darkness, or sadness—that she couldn't quite put her finger on.

"So Arkaroth has a potter, does it?" she said. "How big a town is it?"

"I don't know," he said. "About as big as Ruph? There's an inn, and, well, the usual shops—butchers and so on, and sail and net makers and the boat yard, for the fishing." He picked up another three bowls from Guy's crate and placed them on the shelf.

"Do you have a library in your town?" asked Cory. "We've got a big one by the market; Mumma works in it!"

"No, not one for the town," Daarshan replied. "There's just Coshy Netter, he's got a lot of books. He lets people borrow them if they want."

"Coshy?" Cat cried. "Not Coshy the Poet?"

"I suppose so," Daar said. "He does write poems, and I think he's had some printed." His brows were drawing down in a frown.

"That's amazing! I love his poems. But Yeryl wasn't able to get me his latest book; the book shops in Ilim were sold out already. I'd love to meet him sometime. Do you know him personally?"

"Yes," said the boy. Was Cat imagining it, or was the frown getting more pronounced? "I—my mother—he's a friend of my famil—" Suddenly there was a loud snapping noise, and Daarshan looked down in horror at the

74

two halves of the plate he held in his hands. "I—Master Guy—I'm so s-sorry!" His face was flushed a deep red, and he looked like he was about to cry.

Guy gave the boy a look, then laid a hand on his shoulder. "It's all right, son," he said, taking the broken pieces out of his hands. "That plate was a little warped anyway. You saved me from giving a customer a poorly done piece of work." He gave Daarshan his lopsided grin, then tossed the pieces into the crackpot bin.

"There you go, Frodo," Jamie said, "good job running quality control." He tossed his black bangs out of his eyes and clapped Daarshan on the back.

"Why do you keep calling him Frodo?" asked Cory. "Is that like Papa being called Guy, even though his name really is Dyniselm?"

Out of the corner of her eye Cat noticed that Daarshan looked relieved that the attention had shifted away from his mishap. Had he snapped that plate between his fingers? Cat didn't think she'd seen him apply any pressure, he'd just held it loosely like the other dishes he'd picked up.

Jamie shrugged. "I call him Frodo because he looks like it," he said. "You know, like Frodo in..." Suddenly his face fell, and Cat knew exactly how he felt. He had just been hit with the realization that if he continued his sentence, nobody would know what he was talking about. That he was out of his element, and nobody would get it. Nobody but her, that is.

"From *The Lord of the Rings*? You mean the actor, from the movies?" she asked.

Jamie gave her a grateful look. "Yes! Exactly. It fits, don't you think?"

"I guess it does, at that. No woolly toes, though," she said with a grin.

Guy looked from her to Jamie and back again, a bit puzzled. "Some Outlander joke?"

"Yes, dear," Cat said. "It's from a story in our world."

"Hmph," he said and turned back to his pots. He couldn't be jealous of her rapport with Jamie, could he? Surely he knew better than that.

"What story, Mumma?" Cory said. "You've never told us one about a Frodo!"

"No, I guess not," Cat said. "It's pretty long, and I don't know if I can remember it all that well. But we can give it a try some night. Maybe Aunt Nicky can help us out, or Jamie, if he's still around."

"Yeah, so," Jamie said, clearing his throat, "about that. You said we'd talk about how to get me home. I mean, Edmund was just telling us..."

"Edmund?"

Jamie grinned and nodded his chin in Cory's direction. "Yeah, from Narnia. You know."

Cat did indeed know, and Jamie had a point—her son did look a bit like Edmund Pevensie from the first Narnia film. This kid seemed to think of everyone in movie terms. She smiled at him. "Well, if Cory is Edmund, and Daarshan Frodo, we might just have to start calling you Neo," she said. "Or maybe Ted would work better, you look more like him."

"Huh?"

"You know, from *Bill and Ted's Excellent Adventure*."

Jamie groaned. "Not that guy! I'm not that brainless!"

"Okay, then Neo it is," Cat said. "Keanu Reeves, for sure."

He grinned a bit at that. "Yeah, *The Matrix* is cool. And there was that red pill..."

Guy still had that funny look on his face; even with him half turned away from her and looking at his pots Cat could tell that.

"What red pill?" she asked.

"Uh, never mind," Jamie said quickly, looking a little embarrassed. "What were we talking about?"

"Other than people who look like movie characters? You were just saying Cory told you..."

"Oh, yeah, about those bowls you had. That you came over on." Jamie looked around at the finished pottery on the shelves. "Where do you keep them?"

"The travel bowls? We don't," Cat said. "They got used up. I guess Cory failed to mention that."

"What?" Jamie's face fell. "Da—I mean dang. I thought... What do you mean, they got used up?"

"They were sort of one-way tickets," Cat said. "Well, one-way tickets for two people each. One person was able to go to our world with it, then somebody else came back here on the same one. And then the glaze turned from a bright turquoise to a dull brown, and the bowl no longer worked for travelling. None of those bowls is still around."

"Damn." This time he said the full thing. Not that Cat cared—swearing didn't bother her—but she'd appreciated that he had been trying to be polite before. Now he was too upset to even think about it.

"I know," she said. "I have absolutely no idea how we're going to get you back to our world. How did you get here in the first place?"

Guy's head came up at that, and he turned around.

"Yes, how did you?"

"I'm not really sure," Jamie said. The whole time he had been smacking at the lump of clay in his palm; it had long gone past the nice rounded-mound stage that was of any use for throwing and become something that resembled a petrified cow patty. He looked down at it in consternation, seemed to notice it for the first time, and stuck it back on the work table.

Daarshan picked it up, turned it over once or twice, folded it in half and began to re-wedge it—slowly and a little awkwardly, but with the right motions. "You told Cousin Yeryl about some stones," he said, intent on the clay under his hands, "blue ones. Didn't you?"

Jamie swiped his hair back out of his eyes. "Oh, yeah. Those. I don't even know if that's what did it." He rubbed his palms on the seat of his trousers, leaving a smear of red clay across it, and dug through his pockets. "There." He found what he was looking for in his right pocket, pulled it out and dropped it on the table in front of Cat. Two round stones rolled across the canvas surface. She stopped one from dropping off the edge and picked it up; it was polished to a high sheen, sapphire blue with a white star blazing in the middle.

"Guy!" she said, "look!" She handed him the other one.

He turned it over in his long fingers, then looked up at her. "This is exactly like the ones we..."

"...took off the Slave Masters, back when Andy and Ben first came!" Cat finished. "That's how they travelled across from Chaelia! Where did you get this, Jamie?"

The boy shrugged. "My friend Kaden had them. Well, his sister. And she got them from an old guy who looked like Gandalf."

"Who's Gandalf?" Guy asked.

"Another story character," Cat replied. "Long white beard, big hat and cloak—quite a bit like..."

"Ekinoru!" they said in unison.

"But how could he have..." Guy started.

"...been in my old world?" Cat said. "You know, I wonder. Ekinoru was searching for Andy and Ben, and Ben was taken to our world before he came here. We never did find out how Ekinoru found the boys; he must have been tracing them somehow. I wonder if he followed Ben to my world, left those stones behind, and then came here."

"Who's Eki-whatsit?" Jamie asked.

"The current master of my former apprentice," Guy said. "They all originally came from another world, and used stones exactly like these to travel."

"Another 'other world'," Cat said to Jamie, "not ours. So, what did you actually *do* to make those stones take you over here?"

Jamie twitched up his shoulders. "I don't know," he said. "I don't remember too much about it. Kaden and I were, umm, uh, having, uh, a couple of drinks..." He nervously swiped at his overlong bangs.

Guy raised an eyebrow, then a slow smirk pulled up the corner of his mouth. "Just a couple?"

"Oh," said Cat, "that's what that red pill was all about, huh?"

Jamie shifted back and forth from one foot to the other. "Uh, well, umm..."

"What kind of pill, Mumma?" asked Cory, who had been following this exchange with great interest in his brown eyes.

"Well," Cat said, trying to hide a smile, "there is this story in our world about a man named Neo, and he takes a red pill and goes to another world..."

"And you think that's what happened to Jamie?" the boy asked.

"No, I don't," Cat said. "That's probably not the kind of red pill he is talking about. Is it?" She looked at Jamie, whose mouth was pinched down in a look of acute embarrassment, and took pity on him. "So, regardless of the, uh, state of mind you were in at the time, what precisely did you do with those stones? Just pick them up, and *whoosh*?"

"Pretty much," Jamie said. "Well, I kind of, uh, made a wish. And tapped them together. But it didn't work for going back."

"Hmm," said Cat, "I think we'd better contact Ekinoru and ask about this. But I have an inkling that these might be used up, the way the bowls were." She took both the stones and weighed them in her hand. With Guy's special pottery, which he had only made some very few times, she could usually tell how it worked just by touching it. But there was nothing here; they felt like ordinary smooth stones. She shook her head. "I'm not picking up anything from these. Let's ask Bina, maybe she can feel something. When you say you made a wish, Jamie, did you only wish in your mind, or say it out loud?" Cat spoke the last words over her shoulder as she pulled open the door to take the stones to Bina to check over.

"Umm, I didn't say the wish out loud, no," he said. "Umm, no."

He sounded like there was something he wasn't telling them, something that made him feel self-conscious. What was that about?

Dyllie walked into the workshop.

"Mumma, de goat came down from de roof, an' it's trying to eat one of Papa's socks from de laundry line, and Dola is whacking it with de carpet beater but it won't let go of de sock. Papa, why is Mumma yelling? And what's a infernal four-footed fiend?"

CHAPTER 12

*D*EAR *ANDY, SO THEY* brought me those stones to check, the ones Jamie came over on, Papa said they were exactly like the ones you came on, way back. Mum is writing to Master Ekinoru about it because they think he was the one who gave them to Jamie. Well, not to him, but that's how he got them. Did you ever ask Master E about where he was before he came here to find you? Was he really in Mum's old world? Anyway, I checked those stones, and there is nothing in them now. I could tell that they used to be powerful, but not any more. Mum says that that's what the bowls felt like too, you know the ones, when they got used up.

So, we all talked, and Mum and Papa decided he should try making some new travel bowls. Papa has a little bit left of the Septimus glaze, he thinks it might be enough for two or three bowls. And he said he knows just the ones, three bowls that he made that he couldn't decide what glaze to put on. So they're going to put them in the glost firing and see what happens.

Jamie really wants to go home again. Mum is starting to feel a little bit homesick for Outland, too; the other day she *said "My kingdom for a dishwasher" but when Kell asked what she meant she wouldn't tell him because Papa came in. Papa doesn't like it when she says things like that, he feels worried. He's been feeling worried quite a lot lately, and rushed because of his work, and he and Mum don't have much time to talk. I don't know what to do about it.*

I was at Ben and Liss's yesterday, and they're okay. Still sad, but Aunt says that's how it is, you never forget a baby. Liss still cries a lot, but not as much as at first. She's been pressing some of her milk out, and Aunt gives it to Radyam Black, you know the charcoal burner who lives in the forest off the road to Ilim. It's not much, but Radyam's little girl had a sick stomach, and Aunt says people milk is better for sick little ones than animal, even if they've been weaned. The babies, I mean. Anyway, Liss feels a little better knowing that her milk helps another baby. Mum thinks that's why I felt so strong that Liss shouldn't dry up her milk, because of Radyam's baby, but that's not it. Not really. It's got something to do with Radyam, but not only her baby. I still don't know why, but I know it's important.

But, Andy, that's the other thing. I'm so tired of feeling everything about everybody all the time. I don't even want to go into town any more, because people's feelings just jump on me. It's bad enough at home, with the family, and now there is Jamie and ~~Dar Dahr~~ Daarshan, I'll tell you about him some other day. But right now there's Fionn and the builders, too.

The other day one smashed into his hand with the chisel, and I had the bandages out before he even started cursing up a blue streak (like Mum calls it), because I could feel how much he was hurting. Mum told him to mind his potty mouth around her children, but she didn't really mean it; she was bundling up his hand and trying to keep him from passing out, and she knew talking to him would take his mind off it. It was Damen, you know the big fellow that works for Uncle Chelm in the smithy sometimes, and he can't stand the sight of blood, specially not his own. But Mum talking to him, and a cup of Uncle's applejack, helped him keep it together until he was patched up. Papa says that's good because having a great big lump of a fellow passed out on the kitchen floor would have been ~~incomv inconwe~~ inconvenient to step over to get to the dinner table. But anyway, I felt it right away when Damen got hurt, because he was nearby. I didn't used to feel things quite so much.

I told Mum about it, because I thought she might know what to do, she's Unissima, too. So she said maybe it was because I'm getting older, I'm 11 now, and getting into ~~pewb~~ puberty. She said my Unissima gift took a jump when I was six and lost my teeth and turned from a baby to a bigger kid, so it's to be expected it'll take another jump now. And she thinks maybe I can learn to block it out sometimes, people's feelings, I mean. So I'm going to practise. And I'm practising right now, because there's something going on with somebody, somebody who's in town but I'm not going to tell you who because I'm not thinking about ~~her them~~ it. I don't know what it is, and ~~I don't care~~ I'm practising to not care. I'm sticking my fingers into my feeling ears, Mum said. Like Dyllie puts his fingers in his ears and goes "Lalala!" when I try to tell him it's his turn to do the dishes. Or like hiding under an umbrella that lets all the feelings slide off it. It's easiest when I'm thinking about the people I care about, like Mum and Papa and the boys and you.

I miss you. Lots of love, Bina

PS: (Mum says that's what you put when you forgot something at the end of a letter) I'm sending you some herbs that Aunt helped me mix up, if you put them into some goose grease or lard it makes a cream to help your hands heal if you burn them or cut them, it worked a treat on Damen's hand. I call it Bee's Balm, even though there's no bee balm herb in it at all. Bee's Balm, get it? Love, Bee

PS PS: Aunt Nicky's goat keeps coming back. Jamie calls it Tim the Enchanter, he said it's from a story in their world, one of those movie ones. It made Mum laugh. Love, Bee

CHAPTER 13

"**Y**ow!"

Cat heard Guy's shout right across the front yard. She put down her shopping basket and stuck her head in the workshop door. "What's up?"

Guy stood over a bucket of glaze slurry, shaking the hand with which he had dipped a pot in the mix.

"Ouch!" he said, "there's something that burns in here!"

"What glaze is it?" Cat asked.

Guy stuck his hand in a bucket of water, scrubbing the glaze slurry off.

"The green one," he said. "It's got the black copper in it I got from Sudha Kettlesmith, and beech ash. Andy says that combination worked well for them when they tried it."

"Have you used it before?"

"No, but Andy didn't say anything about it burning."

Daarshan wandered over, a lump of clay in his hand, and looked into the bucket. He got a thoughtful look on his face, put down his lump of clay, stuck his finger in the glaze pot and pulled it back out, carefully studying the glaze that was coating his finger tip. He shook his finger like Guy had done, stuck it into the bucket to wash it off, then gave Cat a slightly distracted look.

"Vinegar," he said. "Have you got any, Mistress Cat?"

Cat raised her eyebrows.

"Of course I do," she said. "Why?"

"It'll fix the burn," he said.

"You mean in the glaze mix, or Guy's hand?"

"The glaze," he said, "but maybe it'll help Master Guy as well."

He was right about Guy's hand—Cat could feel it.

"Vinegar, huh?" she said on her way out the door. "That means it's caustic. Keep that hand in the water, Guy, and make sure you get all that stuff washed off!"

She came back with the brown pottery jug of cider vinegar and a pot of Bina's new salve, the girl in tow. She took Guy's hand, gently dabbing it dry with a towel, then put a glob of ointment on the reddened skin.

"What is this?" Jamie wanted to know.

"Oil, beeswax, marigold, comfrey, plantain and midsummer flower," Bina said. "It's great for burns."

"I'm not a hundred percent sure, but I think midsummer flower is St. John's Wort where we're from," Cat said.

"Oh," Jamie said, watching Daarshan pour a glug of vinegar into the glaze pot.

"Watch it, son," Guy said with a slight smile, "don't spoil my glazes."

Daarshan looked up, startled, as if he was only now becoming aware of what he was doing.

"Oh! I'm—I'm sorry, Master Guy!"

"'S okay, Papa," Bina said, "I think he's right, the vinegar is going to make it not burn."

"All the same," Cat said, "you shouldn't dunk your hands into the glazes. I'm surprised you haven't poisoned or injured yourself before now." Rubber gloves, that's what they needed here—but of course, those didn't exist in Ruph. She finished spreading the ointment on the back of Guy's hand. "It can't be good to have your bare hands in this stuff all the time."

"I have to," Guy said with a slight frown. "There's only so much I can do with pouring the glazes on. I have to dip the pieces—how else am I going to glaze them?"

"Tongs," Daarshan said, then flushed bright red when they all looked at him.

Guy raised one of his eyebrows.

"How do you mean, son?"

Daarshan shrugged, looking embarrassed. "Well, if you had some tongs, like so," he moved his fingers like a pair of pincers, "you could use those instead."

"Good thinking," Guy said. "I'm not sure I have anything like it, though. I wonder if Sepp..."

"The builder guy has a tool like that, some kind of pliers," Jamie put in. "I saw him using it on the nails."

"Yes, he does!" Bina said. "I'll go ask him if we can borrow it." She gathered her red-gold fall of hair into a ponytail, twisted it into a rope and tied it in a knot at the back of her head, then walked out the door in pursuit of Fionn's tools.

Guy gave his lopsided grin at Daarshan. "Well, son, finish what you started, and get that glaze stirred properly.

There's a stir stick somewhere. We'll have to see how this turns out with the vinegar."

Bina returned with the pliers, and gave Daarshan a close look.

"What else do you know?" she asked him. Cat saw the expression on her face—she obviously had been picking up on the boy's feelings again.

He cleared his throat. "Well, umm—maybe if you washed the beech ash first, next time, Master Guy..."

"Washed it?" Cat said. "Yes, that makes sense. When we make soap, we soak the ashes and drain off the water to get the lye. You'd lose the caustic aspect of it. Not sure what it would do to your glaze consistency, but it could be worth a try."

"Of course," Guy said, "I always... Oh! I forgot this time and put the ashes in straight. It's been so busy, next I'll forget my own head. Well done, son, you found the flaw in that glaze." He briefly laid a hand on Daar's shoulder as he passed him, and the boy flushed up again, this time with surprised pleasure. He gave Guy a glance out of his astonishingly blue eyes, then dropped his gaze to the floor, but the pleased smile on his face lingered. Jamie was right, he did look like Frodo. And he seemed terrified of screwing up—desperate for approval, and then surprised if he got it.

"All right," Guy said, "let's try doing this with a tool." He used the pincers to pick up a bowl, dunked it in the glaze mix, and let the excess liquid run off. "Here," he said, passing the piece to Daarshan, "take that wet cloth and wipe the glaze off the bottom. Careful how you touch the glaze; finger marks will spoil it."

Daarshan gave him a gratified look at being trusted with the next step of the process, and he carefully did as he was bidden.

"Why are you wiping it off again?" Jamie wanted to know.

"It'll stick to the kiln shelf otherwise," said Guy, pulling another bowl out of the glaze. "There, that works, doing it with the pincers. I'll have to get one of these for myself." He rubbed his left hand over the back of his right, which was still an angry red from the irritation of the caustic glaze. "All right, that's that lot." He rinsed the pliers in the water bucket and put the lid back on the glaze container, then rolled his shoulders back. "Now for the interesting bit."

He took three small bowls from the back of the bisque shelf, all three the brick-red colour that the terracotta clay took on after the first firing. None of them was very large, no more than six inches in diameter. The one on the top of the stack was an almost perfect little globe with a small round opening, the two underneath a classic bowl shape, one with a flanged-out rim, the other curving in. Guy's work was always beautiful, but Cat had to agree—these were special.

Guy put the pieces on the table, then reached into the cupboard where he kept his glazes and ingredients and brought out a small lidded jar. It had a chain twined across the top, threaded through the loops of the handles and hooked together with a small carabiner, solidly locking the lid in place.

Cat found that her breath had caught a little and she had goosebumps running down her arms. She looked across the work table at Jamie.

"This is it," she said, "the Septimus glaze. It's what made the first set of travel bowls work."

"Whoa," he said, catching the corner of his underlip between his teeth. "You mean—in that jar—that's my return ticket?"

"We hope," Guy said, looking up from where he was unlatching the chain, "but we won't find out until the bowls are finished and fired. Every time I've used that glaze, it's had a different result." He took the lid off the jar, then stirred the contents with a short stick. "Needs more water," he muttered, and topped up the contents, stirring it again. "We'll have to pour this; there isn't enough for dipping."

Cat frowned into the glaze container. There was a slight feeling of unease in the back of her mind; she didn't think the glaze would work for Jamie the way it was. It was like there was something missing. Bina had her brow wrinkled just a little—it seemed she was having similar thoughts. But neither of them appeared to have a better idea for what to do, so Cat shrugged and put her misgivings aside.

She looked at one of the finished pieces from earlier. There was a bare spot in the glaze where the pliers had gripped the piece. "Is that pliers print going to show after it's fired?" she asked.

"Possibly," Guy said. "Don't think it can be helped, though—it's one of the reasons we're doing the special ones like this." He gestured at the large tin bowl that he was setting up to catch the runoff from pouring the glaze.

"If the tongs were shaped differently, it would leave less of a spot," said Daarshan, who was following the proceedings with interest.

"Right again, son," Guy said. "I might get my brother Chelm—he's a blacksmith—to make me a special set of tongs for dipping, with less of a surface that grips the piece. You've got a real knack for thinking of solutions for pottery, don't you? You must know this from home."

Daarshan shook his head. "No," he said, "it just—just seems the thing to do."

"Really?" said Guy. "So your father or mother isn't a potter then? I could have sworn... Pass me the top bowl, please."

A muscle in Daarshan's jaw jumped, but he picked up the little round bowl with obvious care, gently cupping it in his hands.

"What do your parents do, then?" Guy asked, holding out his hand for the dish.

Daarshan's forehead was deeply creased into a frown. "My f-father is a s-silversm—*Ow*!!" With a loud crack, the bowl exploded in his hands.

CHAPTER 14

*D*EAR *A*NDY, SO *D*AAR *broke one of the three bowls Papa was going to make into travel bowls. He was really upset. Jamie got mad when he realized that that was one of his bowls that were going to help him get back home to Outland. But he didn't say anything, thank goodness, just gave Daar a dirty look, and even so, Daar got even more upset. He was going to run out the door; I think he wanted to go hide somewhere. But Papa caught him and said he needed to clean up the pieces, he'd let them drop on the floor, but that was just Papa's excuse to keep Daar in the workshop. He kept his hands on his shoulders—you know how he does, and how it helps people—and talked to him as if it was no big deal the bowl broke, and Daar calmed down again.*

And once he did, and they were going to put the glaze on the other two bowls, he came up with another good idea. I think it maybe had to do with Papa having his hand on his shoulder still. Daar is really good at figuring out what needs to be done to fix a problem, and with how Papa can boost other people's gifts, I think Daar had a <u>brilliant</u> idea. He said to put those used up travel stones of Jamie's into the glaze, and Mum and I knew right away that that was exactly what would make the glaze work for Jamie. Papa gave Daar a funny look and wasn't sure how they could do it, but then Mum thought of the giant mortar and pestle Papa used before for glazes, and found it in the back of the cupboard, and Daar and Papa and Jamie pounded up Jamie's stones and put them in the glaze. Jamie was a little worried, and I think a little sad about giving up the stones, but he wants to go home so bad he's willing to try anything. And I think this is going to work, those bowls are going to be travel bowls again like Mum's and Aunt Nicky's from way back. So right now they're in the kiln; Jamie and Daar are helping Papa with the firing. Mum wants Papa to sleep at least a few hours in the night; he thinks he can let the guys feed the kiln with wood then. So we should know by the day after tomorrow when they unload the kiln whether the bowls work.

So, you know that person I told you about who's in town? It's getting hard to not feel ~~her~~ them, because there's something pretty big going on with her. But I'm trying to block ~~her~~ them out; I want to learn to be able to not feel someone if I don't choose to. Because sometimes, it's too hard. And also, there's some things, Mum says, that aren't my business to know, especially about strangers. It's one thing when it's family, but not when it's other people. ~~Except this is different Except this person is family~~ I'm just trying to keep them out of my head. But there's something ~~she~~ they want badly, and I think I know what it is. But I can't tell you or you'll know who it is, and that's ~~counterper~~ counterproductive to my learning to not feel people when I don't want to.

94

After Papa glazed the new travel bowls, he showed Daar and Jamie the old cups, you know the ones that make everything stronger that's inside them, so they could see what Papa's special pottery is like. And then we showed them Grandmother Urnhild's dancer figures. Mum and I thought it would be okay to show them, even important, for them, I mean, and we were right. Daar felt really warm because we showed him something that is so special and trusted him with a secret. I don't know if he's ever felt special in his life.

Mum was wondering if you could get the new Coshy poetry book in Rhanathon, but then she said it probably would be too expensive to send out. She really wants that book, though. Aunt Nicky got her the last one for her birthday last year, she had it sent from Ilim. She was here earlier today with Ari and Baby Daruka, and the goat followed them all the way from town, and it almost ate Mum's tomato seedlings which were outside to catch some sun. Well, it actually did eat some, but Dyllie saw it, you know how he is with paying attention to animals, and he and Cory saved the rest of them. I hope the ones it ate aren't the striped tomatoes, those are my favourites. And then Cory and Dyllie tied up the goat to a tree, and it ate all the leaves off the branches it could reach and half the bramble bush beside it, and then it chewed on the rope it was tied with and tore it off the tree and got away. It almost got into the garden, but by then Aunt Nicky was leaving and took the goat with her. Papa says he shudders to think what would happen to the goat if it had ate Mum's baby lettuces, but then, he says, roast goat is quite tasty.

I miss you lots. Write me back soon. Love, Bina

CHAPTER 15

J AMIE PACED UP AND down at the back of the cottage. *This was the day.* He'd get to go home today! His return ticket had come fresh off the printer that morning, meaning those bowls that were supposed to work for taking him home had come out of the kiln. Or 'that bowl', rather.

He'd been really pissed when Daar managed to break one of the bowls when they were glazing them. The guy was super-clumsy, and he should have known that the bowl *mattered* to Jamie. But then it turned out it was just as well; there was only enough glaze for the two that were left. So Guy had glazed those two little bowls, with Jamie's stones (all ground up) mixed into the glaze; everybody seemed to think that would work. Two bowls—one to go, one to spare.

They'd put them in the round-domed kiln in the back behind the house, and Jamie and Daar helped fire the thing, keeping it stoked all night. They had to pull out the bricks that walled up the door of the kiln, wearing super-heavy leather gauntlets, and chuck sticks of wood in—hour after hour after hour. You'd been able to see the pots in there, glowing literally white-hot. "Don't look in there long," Guy said, "it'll burn your eyes." He hadn't meant 'burn from the heat' either, but that the light would damage your retina. Pretty crazy.

And then the kiln had to cool down, which took even longer than the firing—they had to wait for almost two days. The pots would crack if you opened the kiln too soon, Guy said. Jamie thought he'd go nuts.

But he had been so impatient, Guy finally took pity on him, and they'd opened the kiln that very morning, with everybody standing around watching. Guy carefully pulled out the bricks; you could feel the warmth coming out of the structure, but nothing like it had been during the firing, when Daar got the front of his hair singed because he got too close to the hole on one of the loads.

Jamie was glad that Guy didn't let Daar handle any of the finished pieces. It wasn't like he didn't trust Daar, but, well—he didn't trust him. Not after what happened to the first of those three bowls. He didn't think Daar could help it, but either the guy had the worst luck, or there was something wrong with his hands. Something magicky. They did seem to have some magic in this place, apart from people travelling back and forth to different worlds, even if they didn't have the wand-waving Harry Potter stuff. Apparently Guy could make and do special things with his hands, on account of being a seventh son of a seventh son. Maybe because Daar was an eighth son, he ended up breaking things? Sort of the seventh son thing in reverse.

So Guy unloaded the kiln—slowly and carefully, with those leather gauntlets on. Jamie almost went crazy, because those special bowls—Septimus bowls, the kid called them—were right in the centre of the stack. Right in the middle of all the other pottery. Walled in with jugs and platters and cereal bowls and about a million mugs. All of which had to come out first. Slowly. And carefully.

Jamie grabbed a stick from the ground and started whacking at the nearest tree with it. *Whack, whack, whack*—back and forth, like the stick was a sword and the tree some kind of attacking knight—*whack, whack*... It was better than diving in there and 'helping' Guy get that stuff out more quickly. He'd probably burn his hands on it anyway. *Whack, whack*...

Cat stepped over and grabbed his arm, stopping him. She smiled at him, like she understood. "Hey, be nice to my apple tree," she said.

Jamie looked at the tree trunk and realized his attack had left a gauge in the bark of the tree where he'd been hitting it. Oops.

"It's okay," Cat said, "look, he's almost got them!"

She was right; Jamie had been able to see something turquoise blue shimmering between the browns and greens of a couple of water jugs. Guy reached for the first of the jugs and lifted it out, and then—

He groaned aloud, and at the same time Cat went, "Oh, no!!"

Jamie looked, and his stomach dropped right down into his shoes. Shards. Completely shattered. Trashed. The bowls were had.

This was the worst feeling of his life. Ever. He turned away, feeling sick.

"No, wait!" Guy said, and Jamie whirled around. Guy carefully reached into the kiln, and his gauntleted hands brought out a bowl, sparkling turquoise in the morning sun. "It was only one of them that blew up! The other one is fine. See?" He held out the little dish to Jamie. "Look, the glaze seems to have worked."

It sure was an unusual glaze colour—a bright turquoise blue, as brilliant as actual turquoise stones, but with an underlying, deeper blue shimmer, the sapphire colour his star stones had had. Jamie reached out his finger to touch it, but Guy pulled it out of the way.

"Don't, you'll burn yourself," he'd said, "give it a little while." He blew on the bowl like he was trying to cool oatmeal.

"It's true," Cat said, "freshly fired pottery is really hot. Here, Guy..." She took off the scarf she had slung around her shoulders, folded it up, and put it on a little stone ledge beside the kiln. "Put it on there."

Guy gently put the shiny little dish on the ledge, and went back to unloading the rest of his ware.

Jamie hovered over the little bowl. "How are we going to know it'll work?" he said.

"I usually can tell," Cat said, "once I touch it. If it works like the old ones, you just have to make contact with it, and if you want to go away, it'll take you." She held her hand a couple of inches over the bowl, as if she was testing the heat of a barbecue. "I think it might be cool enough..." She reached out for the bowl with both hands.

There was a sharply indrawn breath from Guy. "Cat!"

Jamie looked up and saw Guy staring at his wife, his turquoise eyes really stark in his face.

Cat looked back at him with a strange expression in her eyes. "What?"

The kid pushed herself between them. "Papa doesn't want you touching the bowl, Mum," she said. She reached out a finger and ran it lightly along the edge of the dish. "But it's okay, Papa, really." Then she turned to Jamie with a wide-eyed look, the same turquoise as her dad's—the same colour as that bowl. "It'll work," she said, "the bowl will work to take somebody to where they want to go. You just have to make a wish and pick it up." She flicked her long red hair back over her shoulder and gave him a brilliant smile. She'd be a stunner when she grew up, Jamie thought.

"Like wishing on a star, you mean?"

"Yes, like that," she said.

"Hmm," Jamie said. Weird—did it have anything to do with the stones, the way he wished on them?

"So," Cat said, "now that we know it's going to work—yes, Jamie, if Bina says it will, it will; she knows things—how about we don't rush into anything? I'd love to say a proper goodbye to you before you vanish."

Jamie noticed that she wasn't going anywhere near that bowl right then.

"What do you mean, a proper goodbye?"

"Oh, I don't know—how about we have a nice meal this evening? I could pick up some meat in town when I go in this morning. Oh! Speaking of which, I have to get going! Kell! Dyllie! We need to go!" She turned around to Jamie

101

one more time. "So, do we have a deal? Don't touch the bowl until we're all here and can send you off properly. Okay?"

Well, if it was that important to her, Jamie supposed he could wait a few more hours. Now that he was sure—well, fairly sure...ish—that this would get him home, he could afford to take his time for a bit.

So then Cat went off to the library in town for reading lessons with her kids; Guy loaded the cooled-off pottery into a couple of crates for delivery to his customers and took Cory and Daarshan along to help; Lahni, the Down's Syndrome helper girl (or babysitter, or whatever she was), came to take care of the little guy; and the turquoise bowl was carefully parked on the mantelpiece in the house where it would safely wait to take Jamie home that evening.

He'd finished restacking the wood by the kiln, and then just stayed outside—there was no point in hanging around inside, staring at the bowl; it just made him want to grab it and go right there and then. He poked a stick at the bottom of the kiln; the bricks were still warm from the firing. Amazing how long it held onto the heat.

"Jamie!" The Ginny kid—all right, Bina—came bouncing around the corner of the house. "Jamie, the goat is here again! Can you help me take it back to town? Lahni can't look after Yaya and the goat at the same time, and it's already—Oy, you! Get away from the laundry line!" She raced back around the corner of the house.

Jamie rolled his eyes. That stupid goat was a real pain in the ass. It was quite a pretty animal, as far as goats went—white, black and brown, almost a calico pattern, like the cat Jamie'd had when he was little. And it had these enormous horns, which apparently was unusual for a nanny goat, or so Bina said. But it got into *everything*.

Well, at least the Tim-the-Enchanter horns made it easier to drag the stupid animal back to town. It wasn't like it was vicious or anything, just kept wanting to stop every ten seconds and eat stuff by the side of the road, and then they had to yank on the horns again to make it move.

By the time they finally got out of the woods and into town, Jamie had to bite his tongue to not swear out loud in front of the kid. He didn't think Cat would appreciate her learning 'Outlander' curse words—at least not the kind Jamie liked to use; Cat herself had quite a repertoire of creative names she called the damn animal. Jamie suspected that some of them came straight from Shakespeare; he was sure he'd heard 'crook-pated cankerblossom' somewhere in the plays they'd had to read in Grade 12 English. (Not that he'd actually read them; he just got the videos off YouTube. Pretty funny, though, some of that stuff.)

He wiped the sweat from his forehead with the crook of his elbow.

"Where to now?"

The kid let go of the goat for a moment to swipe the back of her hand over the side of her own face.

"Aunt Nicky's—that way," she said, grabbed hold of the goat's horn again and pulled to get it to start moving down the street.

"Maaah!" went the goat and dug in its feet.

"Maaah to you too," Jamie said, "let's go!"

"Maaah!" the goat said right back. Oh man, he was having conversations with a goat. It was high time he went home.

He couldn't wait to be done with stuff like this and get back to civilization. He liked the Weasleys and Daar—they were cool people—but he was fed up with the primitive lifestyle. It all looked so much better on a video game screen than when you had to live it in real life. The goat was a case in point: at home, a farmer would throw the critter into the back of a pickup truck and the job would be done in five minutes. Jamie could—not—wait.

He tugged on the goat's horns again, and for a change it came along willingly. They had reached the marketplace, and there was some major activity going on in front of the big hall, that Tudor-style building with the clock tower on top that stood along one side of the square. About a dozen small leafy trees in tubs, birch trees or something, sat on the cobbled pavement, and a group of workers were arranging them around the sides of the square. A couple of women were decorating them, looping a wide ribbon from tree to tree, and another one was wrapping a different-coloured ribbon around each of the bright green crowns of the eight-foot-high trees. A stage was being roped off in front of one side of the hall door, and trestle tables set up on the other side.

"Oh look!" the kid said, "they're almost ready for the May Day Dance tonight!"

"Some town party?"

"Yes," she said, guiding the goat along one of the small roads away from the market. "It's just for the young people, though. I won't get to go for another year or two, I'm not old enough. My cousin Rhitha could go, she's thirteen, but she's not here right now. And you could go!" She gave him a bright smile.

Jamie almost let go of the goat. "Uh, no, thank you! I don't do dancing."

"Oh, come on! Why not? It's fun! Oh, and Daar could go too!"

Jamie scoffed. "More power to him, then. But not me, no way. Wild goats couldn't drag—hey!"

The goat abruptly stopped and dug in its feet. Jamie got a good grip on the critter's horn and pulled. Its hoofs started to slide over the cobbles, then caught, jerking them to an halt. The goat bucked and shook its head back and forth, catching Jamie a clip on the side of his hip that sent him sprawling into the road.

The kid hung onto the animal with both her hands, but the goat was too strong for her, pushing and shoving her off into a side alley.

"Damn beast!" Jamie tried to jump to his feet, but he had bashed his knee hard on the cobblestones; a sharp pain shot through his leg and he staggered. "Ow!"

Suddenly he saw a figure sidling around the corner of the building, someone in a dark cloak. The person looked around, caught sight of Jamie, quickly turned their head away, twitched the hood further over their face, then hurried down the road in the direction of the forest. Wait—wasn't that the woman from the wagon? The grumpy one, who'd ridden with them almost all the way to Ruph, but got off right before they'd got to town? She'd

105

simply vanished then, but it looked like she'd been around town all this time after all.

Whatever. Jamie carefully put down his foot, realized that the pain had subsided and he could now put weight on it, and hobbled after the kid to help her wrestle the stupid goat to where it was supposed to go.

CHAPTER 16

T HEY HAD ONLY BEEN sitting in Nicky's kitchen for about five minutes; the stupid goat was back in its pen, and Nicky had put on the kettle to make some peppermint tea, which seemed to be the drink of choice in this place—they called it mintbrew. Jamie was just taking his first bite of one of the cookies she'd brought out, when the kid jumped to her feet with a yell.

"What?" Jamie asked.

She grabbed him by the arm.

"Quick!" she shouted, "we've got to go! There's something going on at home, and it's to do with you—come on, quickly!"

Jamie crammed the cookie into his mouth and let her drag him out the door.

"What the heck is going on?" he huffed as they ran through the streets, dodging around corners and slipping on the cobbles.

"It's my—cousin," the kid panted, "her name is—Kashinka—and she's been—in town—ever since you came—too." She ducked between the trees that marked the entrance to the forest path leading to the pottery. "I knew she was—around—but I tried to—ignore it—but now she's about to—do something—and we have to—" Abruptly she stopped. "Wait," she said, with a startled expression on her face as if she'd heard something. "Too late. Drat."

Jamie hunched over with his hands on his bent knees, gasping for air.

"What the heck," he puffed, "so this was all for nothing?"

"I don't know," the kid said, "I think so. There's something that happened; I'm not sure..."

"So what was that about your cousin?" Jamie was slowly catching his breath.

"I knew she was in town," she repeated, flicking her hair back over her shoulder, and taking to the path again at a more leisurely pace. "She left town a couple of years ago, but I think she came back the same day you did."

"Wait a sec'," Jamie said, "is she older—like an adult, I mean, older than you? And does she have dark hair, and a face that could be pretty if it wasn't so grouchy?"

"Yes, that's her," the girl said.

"She was on the cart with us," Jamie said. "And I saw her, earlier, when we were wrestling the stupid goat! I think she went down this path."

"That's what I was afraid of," said the kid. "I think she's after the dancers again—remember, the sculptures we showed you."

"The Chinese ones? What's she got to do with those?"

"They belong to her grandmother, and they're really special—they've got power," the kid said, a solemn look on her face. "Kashinka wants them for the money you could get for them. Remember, we told you about Rhitha and Grandmother Urnhild, and that they left the dancers with us while they're away in Rhanathon at the coast? One of the reasons for that is that we wanted to keep the dancers safe from someone breaking into Grandmother Urnhild's house and stealing them. Kashinka is Rhitha's sister; she thinks she has a right to them. But last time she was here she couldn't get them, so she left town. And now she's back, and I tried to pretend I didn't know it because I didn't want to feel everything about everybody." She pinched her lips together.

"Well, you can't know everything all the time," Jamie said. He didn't quite get why she was upset about this.

"No," she said, still in that little-girl-lost tone, "but this time I did, and I blocked it out. And now something has happened, and we can't do anything about it."

They came out into the clearing with the house and the pottery shop. The door to the house opened, and the Lahni girl stumbled out. She was literally wringing her hands, twisting them in the red-and-white-striped apron she had tied around her waist.

"Oh, Cousin Bina and Cousin Jamie, I was going to ask Cousin Guy 'cause he came back from town and he's in the pottery shop, 'cause I don't know what to do, 'cause Cousin Kashinka came and then she just 'sappeared and I didn't know and I was just gonna show her 'cause Cousin Guy made it and…"

The kid grabbed Lahni's hands and held them still.

"It's okay, Lahni," she said, fixing the older girl with a steady look from her brilliant turquoise eyes, "it's okay. Just tell us what happened. Cousin Kashinka was here?"

Lahni drew a deep breath and bobbed her round head up and down.

"Yes," she said, her eyes big. "First Cousin Guy and Cousin Cory and Cousin Daarshan came home, and they went into the pottery shop and closed the door. And then I was sweeping the floor in the house, because there was dust there from Fionn Builder. And then Cousin Kashinka came in, she didn't knock on the door. But I said hi anyway, 'cause that's polite. And she asked me questions about do I know where Cousin Rhitha and Cousin Urnhild left their things, but,"—a crafty look ran over her features—"I didn't tell 'cause Cousin Cat said not to. But I showed her the bowl, the pretty blue one, 'cause Cousin Guy made it and it's pretty, and she picked it up and she 'sappeared!"

"She disappeared?" the kid said, a shocked look on her face. "What about the bowl?"

"The bowl 'sappeared, too."

A shockwave, burning and freezing at the same time, shot over Jamie from his scalp down his spine and back up again. "WHAT?!?" He bounded over the threshold of the cottage, frantically looking around the room. The spot on the mantelpiece—empty. The big table—empty. The dresser under the window—empty. Empty, empty, empty! His bowl, his ticket to go home, to finally get back to where he belonged—*gone*!!

A red haze descended over his vision, and he whirled around.

"YOU STUPID, RETARDED COW!" he screamed. "THAT WAS MY ONLY TICKET HOME! YOU ID-IOT!"

Vaguely he could see through the red filter over his eyes that the girl looked like he had slapped her in the face, but he didn't care. She'd ruined everything! That dumb retard, she...

Suddenly he was choking, his collar pulled tight by a fist at the scruff of his neck. He felt himself dragged out the door of the cottage and slammed against the side of the house. The fist transferred to the front of his shirt, and Guy's turquoise eyes, level with his own, glared at him with such fury that all at once Jamie's own anger leaked out of him like a punctured water balloon.

"*Nobody—talks—to anyone—in my house—like that!*" The back of Jamie's head thumped against the wall with each word. "*Do—you—understand—me—boy?*"

Jamie, petrified, just managed to nod his head.

Guy's eyes narrowed. "Good. Make an apology to Lahni, and it had better be a good one. Else you can pack your bags and never show your ugly face here again. *Got that?*"

He gave Jamie one more thump against the wall, then let go of his stranglehold on Jamie's shirt, turned on his heel and stomped across the yard into the workshop, slamming the door behind him.

Jamie slumped back against the wall and ran a finger under his collar, trying to get some air. Damn. Damn damn damn. He stabbed all ten fingers through his hair and rubbed the back of his head where Guy had slammed it into the wall. *Damn!* What the hell was he going to do now? His bowl was gone, there were no more stones to make another one—and even if there were, he'd pissed off the one person who'd be able to make it happen. He was out on his ass—he'd be lucky if he could find a place to sleep in the woods. And it was all his own damn fault. What a complete and utter idiot he was. He'd thrown away his home, the place where he belonged; shrugged it off like it was so much garbage, wishing himself away from it—and now that he'd give anything to get back, he'd completely blown any chances of that ever happening.

He sank down onto his haunches, burying his face in his hands.

A small hand touched him on his arm.

"Jamie?" the kid said. "It's okay. Papa'll get over it."

Jamie groaned. "He's kicked me out!"

"No, he hasn't," she said, "he's just mad because you were a jerk to Lahni. It wasn't her fault, you know. She didn't understand."

Jamie rubbed his hands over his face. The kid was right, he'd been a total jerk. Guy had a good reason to hate him.

"He doesn't," the kid said, mindreading again. "Papa just has a temper. As do you, by the looks of it. Come on." She pulled him up by his arm. "Just tell Lahni you're sorry. You know you are."

Jamie followed her into the cottage, his head drooping. What a total, total asshole he was. There had really been no call to treat the girl like that—she hadn't known. And even if she had, she was—was—well, she couldn't help it. But his bowl was gone. This was the suckiest day of his entire freaking life.

Lahni gave him a scared look from her slanted brown eyes, and Jamie's opinion of himself dropped by another dozen hitpoints. Jackass. Jerk. Idiot! Imbecile! Retar—no, not that. He'd never use that word again, ever. How could he have?

"Umm," he mumbled, staring at the mantelpiece behind Lahni's head, "umm, I'm sorry. I..."

"What Jamie means to say, Lahni," the kid interposed, "is that he's sorry he was a jerk and yelled at you. He shouldn't have done that. Right?" She gave Jamie a quizzical look, like a little copper-and-turquoise-coloured bird.

Gratefully, he nodded. "Yeah, what she said. I'm really sorry. That was—was—like—totally uncalled for. I didn't really mean—" He rubbed his hand over his sweating neck. There was no way she would forgive him that kind of insult. "I—oh, da—dang it. Bina's right, I'm a jerk."

Lahni looked at him with her eyes wide, and Jamie could practically see the wheels turning in her head as she tried to comprehend what he'd said. All of a sudden, her face cleared as if the penny had dropped—and what she did next completely floored Jamie. She broke into a big smile and threw her arms around him.

"It's okay, Cousin Jamie!" she said. "And I'm sorry about your bowl, too." She tipped back her head, which was approximately level with Jamie's breastbone, and looked up at him—the sweetest smile he'd ever seen on anyone. His mouth fell open, and awkwardly he hugged her back.

"Uh, thanks," he stammered. "I just, uh, wish I could, uh, make it up to you. I ..."

Lahni let go of him and stepped back. "Friends?" she said, sticking out her hand.

Jamie felt a grin making its way out of the side of his mouth. "Friends!"

The Ginny kid—he really needed to get used to calling her Bina, but it was so much easier to think of her as Ginny—was watching them shake hands with a matching grin on her own face.

"There," she said in a satisfied tone. "So now that we got this sorted out, we can start all over with thinking how we're going to get you home to Outland. I wonder if..."

Jamie's stomach dropped again like he was on some kind of rollercoaster.

"I still don't get what exactly happened," he said, swiping his hair out of his forehead. "What did that cousin of yours—that Ka-Katrina..."

"Kashinka," the Ginny kid said. "I think she came here looking for the dancers. Except Lahni didn't tell her where they are. But she showed her the bowl, and when Kashinka touched it, it took her away—she must have really wanted to leave; that's how the bowls work. They take you if you really want to go. And I think you have to make a wish, too. Did Kashinka make a wish before she vanished?"

Lahni shook her head. "She didn't say anything, just 'sappeared."

"You're not supposed to say the wish out loud," Jamie said. "I mean, that's how..." He broke off, embarrassed. This was kiddie stuff.

The Ginny kid gave him a hard stare. "How do you know?"

He shrugged. He wasn't about to tell her that he'd wished on a star, and that's what got him into this mess—even if the star was just in a blue stone. Which was gone now. And so were the bowls that were supposed to have taken its place. Damn.

"There's something else," the kid said. "About Kashin-ka. We're not done with her, I think."

"Is she coming back?" Lahni looked alarmed. "I don't like Cousin Kashinka. She's mean. And not polite."

"If she's from out of town, how do you know her in the first place?" Jamie asked.

"Oh, she used to live here," the kid explained. "I was still little, but Lahni would remember her from then. And from a couple of summers ago, they were here for a few months. I'm not sure if she's coming back," she said to Lahni, "but don't worry about her, okay?"

"I 'member Cousin Kashinka had a really pretty dress for the May Day Dance once, it looked really shiny and red and soft. But she wouldn't let me touch it. I wish I could go to the May Day Dance tonight," Lahni said wistfully.

The kid scrunched her mouth sideways and let her gaze travel between her cousin and Jamie. Then she grabbed Jamie by the sleeve of his shirt and pulled him outside.

"Hey," she whispered, "you want to make it up to Lahni? You could take her to the May Dance!"

Jamie pulled back. "I can't dance!" he protested. He'd always successfully avoided it—even ducked out of his prom before the dancing started.

"Sure you can, it's easy," she said.

"And I don't have any fancy duds to wear for a party!" Not even at home—when you're six foot two and skinny, suits are hard to come by. His grad outfit had been a pair of black slacks and a white shirt.

The kid looked him up and down.

"Papa can loan you his feast vest," she said. "You're the same height."

No way would Guy loan him his clothes—he hated him.

"I told you, he doesn't," the kid answered his thoughts. She took Jamie by the sleeve again and pulled him over to the workshop.

"Papa, Jamie needs a favour!" she said, bursting through the door, towing Jamie behind her.

Guy looked up from his clay and gave them a deadpan look. "Oh?"

"Yes, he's going to take Lahni to the May Dance!" the kid said.

"No, I'm not! I mean, uh..."

The kid ignored Jamie. "He's going to take Lahni to the Dance, and so he needs to borrow your feast vest!"

Guy raised an eyebrow.

"The May Day Dance, huh?"

"Yes, 'cause Lahni really wants to go and hasn't got anyone to take her!"

"And so *Jamie*,"—Guy drew out the syllables like the name gave him a bad taste in his mouth—"thought of wanting to take her, did he?"

"No!" Jamie squirmed under the potter's ironic gaze. "I don't—I mean, didn't think of it—I mean..."

116

The corner of Guy's mouth twitched.

"And I can't even dance!" Jamie finished up, desperately.

Now Guy was definitely grinning. "Sounds like the perfect penance, then," he said. "Go ahead, Bina, you know where my vest is. I almost want to go watch the dance now; it should be a sight to behold."

Guy grinned again when Jamie walked into the kitchen in the late afternoon, all dressed up in what he was informed was Guy's second-best vest and a pair of his nice pants.

Jamie awkwardly tugged down the vest and cleared his throat.

Cat looked around from whatever she was stirring on the stove. "Looking good," she said with a smile.

He looked like an idiot.

"No, you don't," Bina said, answering his unspoken thought, "Mum is right, you look nice!"

Guy gave Jamie a raise of one eyebrow. "You'll do," he said. "Don't mess up my feast clothes, and don't do anything stupid."

Jamie looked at Daar, who was sitting at the bench by the table. "Aren't you coming?"

Daar looked surprised. "Who, me?" He went a bit red in the face. "I—I don't have any feast clothes, either!"

Again, the Ginny kid had the answer. "We'll go ask Uncle Sepp," she said, "one of his vests should fit you! Come

117

on, put on your clean trousers, and we'll go!" She tugged Daar by the sleeve to get him up from the bench.

He threw one of his worried Frodo looks at Guy, like he was asking if it was okay. Guy gave him a nod.

"Go ahead, son," he said. "I'm sure my brother won't mind lending you a vest. And besides, you can keep an eye on *him*,"—he cocked an eyebrow at Jamie—"make sure he keeps his word."

Cat laughed. "Don't listen to Guy, Daarshan," she said. "You go if you want to; never mind policing duties."

Frodo looked confused. "What duties?"

"Oh," said Cat, "policing is like beadle's work—dealing with lawbreakers. What I'm saying is, go or don't go because you want to, not because you think you have a duty."

Jamie wished he had that option; he'd be out of those fancy duds and back on that kitchen bench like a shot.

"No, you don't, Jamie!" the Ginny kid said, her hands on her hips. "You promised Lahni, and she's so looking forward to it! Okay, Daar, you coming?"

Daar shrugged with a slight smile on his face. "All right then," he said. "Sure, might be fun."

No, it wouldn't. It'd be a pain in the ass. Jamie tugged on the vest again as he watched Daar walk out the door to change his pants.

CHAPTER 17

J AMIE JIGGLED NERVOUSLY FROM one foot to the other. They'd arranged that he'd meet Lahni in front of the library, but now he was wishing he got directions to her house instead. At least then he wouldn't have to stand here right across from the hall, trying to hide behind one of those silly beribboned potted birch trees so he wouldn't be so obvious to the party crowd that was already starting to mill around on the market. He was sure he stuck out like a sore thumb—everybody seemed to know everybody else in this town. And where was Daar? The kid had taken him off to her uncle's to borrow some clothes, and there was no sign of either of them.

That little stage in front of the hall was now occupied with a band—no electric guitars and synthesizers, of course, but they did have some serious drums there, manned by an older black guy who was already raising quite the rumble from the big kettle drum in front of him. There were also a couple of younger people with some sort of round-bellied guitar-type things, at least three fiddlers (their instruments were also more rounded, not the curvy violin shape that Jamie was used to), and a few musicians with wind instruments. Judging by the squawking sounds one of those made, Jamie figured it was some kind of clarinet, but it looked different from the one he'd played in band class in school—more like a recorder, with holes instead of the silver keys his used to have. The band was tuning up with the typical squeaks, bleeps, plink-plonks and up-and-down scales that musicians everywhere seemed to produce to warm up.

Jamie ran a finger under his shirt collar. Why hadn't he asked Cat, or even Daar, what type of dancing they did here? If this was anything like ballroom dancing, he was doomed. In Grade 10 PE class they'd made them take dancing lessons, and Jamie still cringed at the memory, especially of the look on Chloe Miller's face when he stepped on her toes, and they'd crashed into Brendan Slater and Surjit Kapoor trying to do the waltz. The next class when he had to choose a partner, every one of the girls had had that look on her face that said "Please don't pick me," and every time after that when it was ladies' choice they'd all bypassed Jamie unless he was the only guy left other than Josh McDonald, who was tone deaf and had zero sense of rhythm. Painful wasn't even in it—dancing just wasn't his scene.

He looked around, wondering if there wasn't some way of weaselling out of this. Maybe Lahni wouldn't come; maybe she'd changed her mind? She hadn't showed up yet, and he'd been there at least five minutes. No, ten. Probably fifteen. A faint hope stirred in his chest. Why would she want to go with him, anyway? There were enough other people here she'd have a lot more fun with. Maybe he could just, you know, sort of make himself scarce...

But then Cat's face flashed in front of his mind's eye. She'd be disappointed, and look it too. And Guy, he'd think Jamie was a loser—again. He'd probably think that he'd been right all along, and he should have kicked Jamie out after all.

And most of all, Jamie's inner vision showed him the Ginny kid, with her hands on her hips and that glare that could laser through steel. She'd skewer him. In fact, that vision was so vivid, Jamie could almost see her for real, coming towards him across the market square...

Oh, no, this was a different red-headed girl altogether. She did look a bit familiar, but she was towing a guy by the hand that Jamie didn't recognize.

"Hello!" the girl called out. Jamie looked behind him, but there was nobody there. Was she talking to him? Apparently she was—she kept coming straight at him. She looked to be about Jamie's own age, maybe a bit older, and had most of her hair piled on top of her head, with a few strands trailing down the sides, and flowers stuck all over it.

"Aren't you staying with Uncle Guy and Aunt Cat right now?" She did a little curtsy-bob. "I'm Kimira, I think you met my sister Liss." Ah, that's why she looked familiar. "And this is Kaltas," she said, dragging her boyfriend forward.

"Hello," said the guy with a friendly grin, giving Jamie a little salute with two fingers. "My father is working on your house right now—the Septimus house, I mean. Fionn Builder."

"Nice to meet you," Jamie said, feeling awkward. Was he supposed to do that funny bow Daar always did when he met people?

"Are you here by yourself?" Kimira asked. She didn't seem to expect anything from Jamie he wasn't doing, so that was a relief.

"Uh, no," he said, "I mean, uh, yes, right now, but I, uh, I'm meeting someone. A—a girl called Lahni."

"Oh, you're taking Lahni? That's great!" She beamed at him, then looked past Jamie's shoulder. "Look, there she is now!"

Jamie turned, and there indeed was Lahni, coming across the marketplace with her mother. She was wearing a bright red shiny dress that made Jamie think of a candy apple. It was sort of poufy at the top and drapey at the bottom, ending somewhere around her knees, with a sash thing around it that swung back and forth as she came skipping up to them.

"Hi, Cousin Jamie!" she said, a big smile on her round face and her eyes sparkling. "Mumma brought dough dabs, and she's going to put them on the food table, and we're going to dance! Hi Cousin Kim and Cousin Kaltas! Look, the musicians are already getting ready to play!"

"Hello, Jamie," her mother said with a good-humoured smile. "Now that I've delivered this chatterbox to you, I'd best take these to the food table. Here, have one." She held out her dish which was piled high with little brown pastries that looked like pillow-shaped donut holes. "It's real kind of you to take my girl to the dance; she's not stopped talking about it since she got home!"

Now he felt like a real shmuck for even considering standing Lahni up. Good thing he hadn't given in to temptation. "It's, uh, it's okay, uh, I mean, you're welcome!" he stuttered, running his finger under his collar again.

"Try one of Mumma's dough dabs, Cousin Jamie! They're really yummy!" Lahni held out one of the pastries to Jamie and smiled up at him. "You look real handsome, Cousin Jamie!"

Jamie couldn't help it, he had to smile back at her. "And you're looking really pretty," he said. What was more, he meant it. Usually Lahni wore her hair loose, pulled back from her face with one of those Alice-in-Wonderland headbands, but today she had it kind of rolled and pinned up around the back of her head, with little yellow and blue and white flowers stuck all along it, and woven through it a candy-apple-red ribbon that matched her dress, the ends fluttering down her back. She looked sweet, and not only because of the candy apple connotation, either.

He popped the dough dab in his mouth; as he'd suspected, it was exactly like donut holes, the fresh-baked ones you got at the stall at the fall fair at home. "You're right, this is really good," he said around the crumbs before he'd even swallowed it.

"Let's go see what else there is to eat!" Lahni grabbed Jamie by the hand and started pulling him towards the food table. "And to drink, there's good things to drink there! Cousin Sardor made a special cider just for today, and the May Bowl! It's got woodruff in it!"

"Good idea," Kaltas said, "I'm getting thirsty. I've been looking forward to Sardor Brewmaster's May Bowl all week."

"I love how you've done your hair," Kimira said to Lahni as they walked across the square. "How do you get the flowers to stay in? Mine always fall out."

"Mumma did it for me! She..."

Kaltas looked past the chattering girls' backs at Jamie and rolled his eyes upwards in a show of male solidarity. Jamie felt a grin make its way past the corners of his mouth. Maybe this wouldn't be so bad after all.

They stopped about a dozen times on their way to the food tables, because Lahni had to say hello to everyone.

"Hi, Cousin Mahadev, this is Cousin Jamie, he's visiting from Outland! Hi, Cousin Lilla, this is Cousin Jamie! Hi, Cousin Amr! Hi, Cousin Nerit! Hi, Cousin Torrence! Hi..." By the time they got to the punch bowl, Jamie had been introduced to what seemed like a hundred people, all of whom Lahni called 'cousin' and told that Jamie was a visitor from Outland. He got a few curious looks, but mostly friendly ones, smiles from the girls and some back slaps from the guys. Teenagers seemed to be just the same in Ruph as they were back home in Canada—if anything, friendlier.

A burly grey-haired man presided over the drinks table, dishing out punch from a big bowl that had some bundles of greenery floating in it.

"Hi Cousin Sardor, this is Cousin Jamie, he's visiting from Outland!"

"Hah, so you're the fellow young Bina has been telling the Wife about!" the man boomed. "Welcome to Ruph, son." He engulfed Jamie's hand in a crushing handshake, then passed him a cup of punch.

Jamie took a sniff. Whoa—this smelled like booze!

"Uh, what's in this?" he asked. He wasn't too keen on getting drunk any more—that last time in Hallie's store was going to last him a lifetime.

"Can't tell you that," the brewmaster said with a wink, "but other than the woodruff, there's some sweet and hard cider. But not too much of that. Mostly sweet."

Jamie tasted it. Ah, yes, it wasn't all that strong. It pretty much tasted like apple juice with a bit of fizz, and some other interesting flavours Jamie couldn't identify.

Lahni grabbed his hand again.

"Come on, Cousin Jamie, the dancing is starting!"

He dumped the drink down this throat. Maybe a bit of booze in his system wouldn't come amiss.

Daar showed up again sometime during the early parts of the dancing, wearing a dark blue vest with embroidery around the edges that was even looser around the chest than Guy's was on Jamie—Sepp was built on rather broader lines than Daar—and he'd found himself a girl to dance with, another redhead in a bright blue dress that matched his Frodo eyes. He looked like he was having fun.

And Jamie wasn't surprised, because the dancing completely turned his expectations on their head. Ballroom dancing? Not even close! Sure, there was music, and they moved to it—but that's where the resemblance ended. This was toe-tapping, thigh-slapping music that had them all hopping in a line, twirling in circles, jumping right and stepping left, doing swing-your-partner-round-the-bend, doe-si-does and one-two-threes—far more like a hoedown than a ball. Everybody seemed to do everything in big circles or lines, following what the couple at the front was doing, or not, and having a blast doing so.

In fact, that seemed to be the chief purpose of this, to have fun and laugh your head off. Jamie actually stepped on Lahni's toes, but before he could get out an apology, she went off into a peal of laughter and just kept galloping along sideways down the line in that Virginia Reel dance they were doing at the moment, and when they crashed into another couple at the end of the line, she laughed even louder, and so did the other pair. So what could Jamie do but laugh along?

He forgot all about the fact that he hated dancing, and that he didn't want to be there, and even that he was miserable about the lost bowl, because he was having too much fun. Lahni was beaming the whole time as she hopped and skipped and twirled through the dances, and dragged him to the food table during the pauses in the music, and pulled him back onto the square when the dances struck up again.

And then Jamie took himself completely by surprise by teaching them all the Chicken Dance.

It was Lahni's fault—one of the circle dances had them swinging each other around, and at the end she did a flap with her elbows, which made Jamie laugh so hard he could barely catch his breath. And when he told her why, she dragged him over to the musicians, who were taking a break, so he could sing the tune for the clarinet guy ('Cousin Yaqu'), who picked it up in no time flat.

The next thing Jamie knew, he had the whole square full of dancers flapping their chicken wings, thumbs tucked into their armpits, and wiggling their butts and swinging each other around in the most enthusiastic rendition of the Chicken Dance he'd ever seen. And when it got faster and faster at the end, he and Lahni were the only ones left standing, breathless with laughter at their super-speed chicken wing flapping, and they got a huge round of applause when it ended with a big crash of the kettle drum.

That's when Daar came up to Jamie and told him his awesome idea.

CHAPTER 18

*D*EAR ANDY,

    we're going on a trip! Papa, Mum, Jamie, Daar, Cory, Yaya and me. Yaya is coming because he needs Mum, and I'm coming to help look after him. Not that Cory couldn't do that, but he said he didn't want to (I asked him to say that), so Mum said they'd best take me, too. She was winking at Papa when she said it, because she knows, but it doesn't matter, so long as we both get to come. Cory is going so he'll learn more about glaze materials. And Jamie because it's his stones, and Daar—Sorry, I better start over.

    It was all Daar's idea. You know how I told you he's good with figuring out what to do when there's a problem? Mum says he's a born trouble-shooter. And I told you that Kashinka disappeared with the last travel bowl (Mum and me think she might have gone to Mum's Outland, like my born mother back when I was a baby), and Jamie is stuck here without a way to get home because the blue stones they put in the glaze for the bowls are gone. So at the May Day Dance, Daar was dancing with Cousin Yerina, and her blue dress made him remember that near Arkaroth, that's his home town, there's a place where there are really special rocks, blue-veined ones. He says not a lot of people know about them, and he thinks they could be the same kind of stones as the ones Jamie used for travelling, they're the same colour, he says. So he and Papa think that maybe they can make a new glaze for travel bowls for Jamie out of them, and Mum and me think they're right.

The other thing is that Daar says the potter in Arkaroth uses the sand from the beach in her clay and glazes, so then Papa wanted to go talk to her and maybe bring back some of the sand. And when they were all talking about going on this trip—it was just Papa, Daar and Jamie then—Mum started feeling sad. Then Cory was begging Papa to let him come too, and Papa said to Mum "Might be a good idea," and Mum agreed even though she was feeling even sadder because she was being left out. Right then, there was a huge rattling and banging sound from Fionn and the builders, huger than the noise they'd been making all morning already, and Mum ~~thru~~ threw her hands up in the air and said "I can't stand this racket any longer!" And then Papa looked at her and said "Well maybe you should come too."

So that's why we're all going. And Mum is really ~~cksi cxi~~ excited that she'll get to meet Coshy the Poet, and to get out of Ruph for once. Kell and Dyllie are staying with Aunt Nicky and Uncle Sepp, and we're borrowing Uncle's wagon. Papa is going to drive, and Daar and Jamie are going to help, and Cory wants to learn too. Jamie said Cory is too young for a driver's licence, and Mum laughed and said it hardly matters when you're going no more than 2 miles per hour. She's so happy to be going on this trip, Andy!

So we'll leave the day after tomorrow, first thing. Kelett Carter says it should take us about two days, that's how far Arkaroth is from here. We can go in a direct route to the sea, we don't have to go around the long way down to Ilim and then over the plains and along the coast, which is the way Daar said he came. I don't know if I can write you while we're on the trip, but I'll try.

Lots of love, Bina

PS: There's still something going on with Kashinka, some unfinished business, Mum would call it. I know she's gone, but it's like she left a thing behind. I'm not sure what, and I tried so hard to block her out that I can't pick up on it now, no more than a little bit. I know it's small, whatever it is. And I can't do anything about it while we're going to Arkaroth, so I just hope it'll be okay. Lots of love, Bina

CHAPTER 19

"ARE YOU ABSOLUTELY SURE there aren't bears in these woods?" Jamie said for the second or third time, nervously looking over his shoulder.

"No," said Guy, "but I'm as sure as I can be that if there are any, they'll stay far away from our fire." He poked a long stick at the crackling flame, stirring up the logs.

"I'm sure there's *something* out there," Jamie said. "It's been following us for the last couple of hours at least. There!" He jumped up from the log he was sitting on. "D'you hear that? Something cracked!"

"Well, this *is* the woods," Guy said. "There are bound to be some animals out there."

"Yes, but this keeps following us! Something's after us!"

"It's okay," Bina said sleepily. She was leaning against Cat's arm. Yaya was on Cat's lap; he had snuggled himself to sleep and was drooping over her arm, out cold. Guy was on her other side, his arm wrapped around her, warm and comforting. "Don't worry about what's out there, Jamie," the girl continued, "whatever it is, it won't hurt us."

"How do you know?" Jamie said. He settled down onto his log again and leaned back against the wall of the shelter.

Cat was glad there were traveller's shelters along these roads, about every ten to fifteen miles. This one was a rough structure, more like a small barn or stable than anything else, with fodder for the horse and a stall for it to rest. Not much for the humans—you had to bring your own provisions and blankets—but at least it was a roof to shelter under in the night. If Jamie was right and there was some creature after them, Cat, for one, preferred being indoors with some solid walls around her.

"Bina just knows," Cory put in. He tipped his head back and looked up at the patch of sky that was visible between the tops of the trees. "Look, there's the first star!"

"Where?" Bina said.

"Right there!" Cory pointed. "Star light, star bright," he chanted, "The first star I see tonight..."

"I wish I may, I wish I might," Bina chimed in, and together they finished, "Have the wish I wish tonight!"

"I want Andy to come back," Bina said, and at the same time, Cory called out, "I want to see a dragon!"

"You're not supposed to say your wish out loud," Jamie said, "it'll never come true that way!"

The kids looked at him, astonished, then turned to Cat with an accusing look in their eyes.

"You never said that, Mum!" Bina said in an outraged tone.

"That's because I didn't know," said Cat with a smile.

"I thought everyone knew that," Jamie said. "But we can test it by the scientific method: did any of your wishes on a star ever come true?"

"No-o-o-o..." Cory said.

"See, mine did," Jamie retorted, then clamped his lips together as if he'd realized he'd said something embarrassing.

"Oooh!" said Bina, "that's how you got here! But it wasn't a real star, only the ones in those stones."

He shrugged, going a bit dark in the face. "Yeah, but how did you know?"

Cory shook his head. "Like I said, she just knows. Pass me another apple, Daar."

The young man fished a wrinkled apple out of their food bag and tossed it across the circle. Cory speared it on the end of his stick and held it over the coals.

"Why would Ginny know about all this stuff?" Jamie said. "I'll have another one, too, please." He held out his hand for an apple, and when Daarshan passed him one, took a bite.

"She just does, she's Unissima Maxima," Cory said. "Why do you keep calling her Ginny?"

"It's from a story—" Cat and Jamie said at the same time.

Cat laughed. "Another story from our world," she finished. "You mean Ginny Weasley from *Harry Potter*, right?"

"Yeah," Jamie said with a slightly embarrassed grin, "from the first couple of movies. Sorry, kid."

"I don't mind," said Bina, "at least, I don't think I do. That's the story you told us about the wizard boy, right, Mum? And Ginny is Ron's sister, and Harry's friend."

"Girlfriend, in the end," Jamie said with a smirk.

"Oh, is she?" Cat said. "I never got the full story; the last book hadn't come out when I came here. I've always wondered how it ends."

"Did you see the movies?" Jamie asked.

"Only the first three—or was it four? They were really well made," Cat said.

Guy gave her a sideways look, and the arm that was wrapped around her twitched a bit, like he was having a spasm. At the same time, Bina leaned forward and looked across Yaya on Cat's lap at Guy, then up at Cat, with a rather searching expression in her eyes. Then she tipped her head sideways a little, her brow cleared, and she smiled, leaning back against Cat's arm.

"So what happened at the end of the story?" she asked Jamie. "Mum only told us up to—how far was it, Mum?"

"*The Half-Blood Prince*," Cat said. "And I probably forgot a whole lot of the details, and mixed up other ones. But I always wondered what else happened, how the story finishes up. It's one of the things I regret leaving behind in our world." Guy's arm twitched again. "So Ginny gets together with Harry in the end?"

"That'd be telling," said Jamie with a grin.

"Well, then tell already!" said Cory, raising his chin from his hand where he'd been resting it while he was slow-roasting his apple with the other hand.

"Me?" said Jamie, surprised.

Bina laughed. "Of course you, who else? Mum just told you she didn't know the end of the story. What's the last part of it called?"

"It's, umm, oh—*The Deathly Hallows*," Jamie said.

Cory settled his chin back on his hand, turned his apple stick over the coals, and fixed his brown eyes on Jamie's face. "What's a deathly hollows?"

"Hallows," said Jamie. "They're, uh, these objects..."

"Why don't you start the way the story starts, in the book?" Bina said. "That's how Mum does it."

"That's how I pretend to do it," Cat said with a smile. "They never know the difference, because they don't have the real book to compare it to."

Jamie looked down at his feet. "I, uh—"

All of a sudden Cat realized what his problem was.

"Book or movie, either one," she said. "Like I said, we'll never know the difference; all we want is the story. So, come on, don't keep us in suspense. Please?"

"Well, uh..." He stared into the fire, the flickering light of the flames reflecting off his face, and his eyes took on a faraway look. "It starts with a pair of eyes, and then a voice..."

It was at least three hours later when Jamie's voice finally gave out. Cat drew a deep breath and looked around the circle. The light of the dying embers glittered on the tears that were running down Bina's cheek, shed for the little house elf who so bravely died rescuing his friends. Cory's eyes were closed, his head leaning against Guy's shoulder, but the rhythm of his breathing told Cat that he was awake and had heard every word of the story. Now he slowly opened his eyes and blinked.

"That's not the end of the story, is it?" he said, his voice sounding rough as if he had just woken from a dream.

"No," said Jamie hoarsely, "only of the first movie. They split it in two." He coughed.

"Here," said Daarshan, who had not made a sound the whole time, just looked at Jamie with his big blue eyes, taking in the tale. He handed Jamie his water bottle. "You are a very good storyteller."

"Yes, you are," said Cat. "That was almost as good as watching the movie ourselves. Better, actually. Have you ever done any writing yourself?"

Jamie shook his head and took another gulp from Daarshan's water bottle.

"Well, you should," Cat said. "You're good."

Jamie shook his head again. "Nah," he croaked. "I'm crap. Almost failed English 12. Can't spell worth a dam-sorry, darn."

"So what?" Bina said. "Papa and Cory are dys-dyslec-tic—"

"Dyslexic," Cat corrected.

Jamie's head popped up, and he stared at her.

"Yeah, that," Bina continued. "Mum says they can't spell their way out of a wet paper bag—"

Guy laughed. "Truth, that," he said.

"See?" Bina said. "But it doesn't matter, because Cory is the best storyteller of all of us. Spelling doesn't have anything to do with telling stories, does it, Mum?"

"No, not really," Cat said. "Nor does reading, for that matter. It's far more import—*What the heck was that?*"

They all twisted around and stared into the darkness of the thicket behind them. A loud rustling and crackling came from the bushes. *Was* there a bear? Cat clutched Yaya closer to her.

"Guy! What is that?" She struggled to her feet, ready to run for shelter.

Guy stood, interposing himself between her and the bushes, his arms stretched out to shield the children. The two older boys were on their feet as well, Daarshan clutching a stick of firewood, ready to strike.

The noise came closer and closer, something breaking through the underbrush, something heavy, something—

"Maaaaah!" came a loud cry, and into the light of the fire stepped Nicky's goat.

CHAPTER 20

T HE CART CREAKED SLOWLY down the hill towards Arkaroth. Guy leaned on the brake—a foot-operated lever that applied wooden brake shoes to the wheels—and hauled back on the horse's reins to keep it from breaking into anything faster than a walk; having the cart run away on them on this steep path was a scary thought. Cat and the kids (and the goat, which had been following them all the way from the campsite) were walking to keep the weight off the cart. The only one left riding was little Yaya, who was bouncing up and down on the seat beside Guy, clutching the edge of the wagon with one hand and pointing excitedly with the other.

"Mumma, Mumma, Mumma!" he called, "Mumma, the o-see-ahn, the o-see-ahn!"

"I know, sweetie," Cat said, drawing in a blissful breath of the salty sea air. "Isn't it beautiful?"

Beside her, Bina's eyes were big. "That's not beautiful," she said with awe in her voice, "it's *glorious*!"

The town was spread out below them, an amphitheatre with the bay as its stage. A fleet of fishing boats bobbed in the waters sparkling in the afternoon sunlight, and the dark grey houses were sprinkled up the hillside like crumbs on a pregnant woman's belly.

"Look at all the ships, Mumma!" Cory called out. "They look exactly like our toy ones in the creek at home! I thought they'd be much bigger."

"They're bigger closer up," Jamie said, "the houses are tiny from up here, too. Which one's yours?" He turned to Daarshan.

The other boy gave him a look with his eyebrows drawn down in a frown, but he pointed.

"On the market," he said. "The one by the far edge, facing the harbour, with the pointy gable in the middle."

"The one with the flag on the roof?" Jamie said. "I thought that was, like, city hall or something."

Daarshan shrugged and turned his head away, a look of discomfiture on his face.

Jamie had a point, Cat thought—the house Daarshan had indicated was the largest one of the buildings surrounding the marketplace, which was sprawled out along the top of the tall retaining wall hemming in the harbour bay. The house's central gable was topped by an ostentatious little turret from which a red-and-black banner fluttered in the sea breeze.

"Is that a bell tower?" she asked, then regretted her question when she saw the uncomfortable expression on Daarshan's face.

"Yes." He gave another shrug, as if to say he had nothing to do with his family's choice of building.

"Come on!" Bina called, skipping ahead of the cart. "We're almost there!"

"Last one down is a rotten egg!" Cory shouted and ran to get in front of her, racing down the steep road.

"Wotten egg!" Yaya cried, bouncing in his seat.

"Be careful!" Cat called after them. "Watch that you don't tri—"

"Maaah!" The goat butted her in the hip, sending her stumbling, and bounded after the children.

"Ow!" Cat caught herself on the cart just in time. "That blasted—" she exploded, then clamped her lips shut to keep the swear words she wanted to spit out from the kids' ears.

"Are you all right, Mistress Cat?" Daarshan was beside her, his hand out to steady her by the elbow.

Cat took a deep breath and blew it out again slowly.

"Yes, thank you," she said. "It just caught me off guard, that's all."

"Here," the boy said, thrusting his walking stick at her, "this'll help."

"Thank you!" Cat said, surprised. Then she gave a light laugh. "Do you mean 'help with beating the goat'?" she said. "I could use that right now."

A chuckle escaped Daarshan, and the gloomy expression on his face gave way to a grin that lit up his blue eyes. "No, I meant with walking," he said, "but if you really want..."

Guy had his head turned, looking around at them, and he now gave Daarshan his lopsided grin. "Thank you, son," he said. "I'm so glad to have you along to defend my wife from wild beasts when I'm stuck up here holding the reins of the cart." There was a serious undertone to his words that told Cat both of his chagrin at having been unable to help her, and his relief that she had come to no harm.

She gave him a smile, then looked from him to Daarshan. Once again the boy had that look in his eyes that showed how deeply he was moved by Guy's approval, even though it was expressed as half a joke.

"Goat kebabs!" she said. "If that 'wild animal' doesn't watch it, I'm going to start looking for recipes. Roast goat, goat fricassee, goat cutlets…"

"Goat stew sounds good," Guy added, giving Daarshan a wink. He had seen the look on the boy's face, too.

"I like goat meat on a stick, roasted over coals," Daarshan said, obviously getting brave.

"Oh yeah, barbecued goat," Jamie said, "great idea. Hey, how about goat burgers, with pickles and bacon and melted cheese?"

Cat laughed. "Yes, but for the cheese we'd have to keep the goat around; we'd need the milk."

"It doesn't have milk, though, does it?" Jamie said. "Or were you supposed to have milked it or whatever?"

"No, she's too young," Cat said. "They have to have kidded first—given birth, I mean—before they start giving milk. Thank goodness this one hasn't yet; if we had to milk the silly thing to boot…"

"No kidding," Jamie said with a grin.

Cat groaned and rolled her eyes at the lame pun. She was leaning on Daarshan's walking stick as they were making their way down the hill—it really did help on that steep

141

road, and she was glad for the support of the stick as she could feel the bruise on her hip where the goat had banged into her. They were close enough to town now to hear the roar of the surf and the cries of the seagulls soaring over the harbour; the air held the tang of seaweed and the smoky scent of the cooking fires in the houses.

They came to a junction, a smaller side path joining the main road from the right. Steps crunched over the gravel, and around the bend in the path a young man came striding into view. He was fairly tall, with blond hair swooping back from a strong cowlick on his forehead, and had a coat slung by one finger over a well-muscled shoulder, whistling a jaunty tune as he walked. Looking up, he caught sight of them, and without missing a note in his tune raised his hand and waved a greeting.

But abruptly, the tune broke off, and the young man's jaw dropped. Cat became aware that Daarshan at her side had stopped in his tracks.

Then the stranger broke into a delighted grin.

"Squirt!" he cried, and he ran the last few paces to meet them. "Shrimp! What brought your puny little face back to the old home town?" He dropped his coat, caught Daarshan around the neck and rubbed his knuckles in his hair. "Couldn't stand it without us, could you? Had to come back to the home fires, eh?"

Daarshan fought free of the headlock, then with a grin on his face slapped the other on the back. "It's not you I was missing!" he said. "I had to come home to remind myself how much better life is away from this hole in the ground." The young man punched him on the arm, and

Daarshan punched him right back. "So, you're still chasing after Sinya, are you?" He gestured down the road the other had come from.

The young man turned to Daarshan with an eager expression in his face. "You haven't heard yet, Shrimp!" He exuberantly clapped Daarshan on the shoulder. "No, you wouldn't, you left before then! Well, get this, Puny!" He puffed out his chest. "You are looking at a betrothed man!"

Daarshan snorted, but his mouth was twisted into a wry grin. "So she finally said she'd have you, did she? Good for you. Took you long enough." He gave the young man another slap on the arm. "Only betrothed, though, not married? What are you waiting for?"

The other turned a little red in the face. "Father is building us a room at the back of the house. And Sinya's mother wants her to wait until I have a home to take her to, so we had better. But it won't be long, no more than a few months! We'll have the celebration on summer solstice; Father has promised to have our rooms ready by then. We're going to have the one at the back of the house, too, the one that... Oh." He broke off.

Daarshan's face had folded down into a frown again. "The one that used to be mine, yes."

The young man awkwardly cleared his throat and rubbed the side of his nose with his forefinger. "Well, I—we—"

"Don't worry about it." Daarshan kicked at a small rock with the toe of his boot.

"So who's this you're with, Tiny?" the other said quickly, obviously trying to change the subject.

Daarshan looked up. "Oh! Sorry!" He turned to Cat. "Mistress Cat, Master Guy, this is my brother, Jarin Septimus. Jar, this is Cousin Kaltbur's wife's-brother and his family, and Jamie, he's a friend. They've come here to..."

"To meet Father!" the young man eagerly concluded, as he made a leg. "I'm honoured to meet you, cousins."

Guy held out his hand. "Pleased to make your acquaintance." Cat noticed he didn't bother to correct Jarin's assumption as to the purpose of their visit. She shook the young man's hand as well—he had a solid, confident grip—and then Guy set the horse in motion again.

Another fifteen minutes of walking brought them to the edge of town, the cart rattling over the cobbles in the narrow road between the houses. The kids were looking around curiously.

"Why do the houses all have those dark shingles stuck on the side, not just on the roof?" Cory asked.

"I would imagine it protects the house walls from the ocean winds," Cat said. "Look, on most of the houses the ocean-facing side is completely covered in siding—that's where most of the weather would beat against it; the other sides of the houses only have the top half shingled."

Jamie ran his fingers over the tiling on the house they were passing. "What is this stuff, some kind of stone?"

"Slate," said Daarshan.

"That's what I thought," said Cat. "You must have a lot of it around here."

"Sitting on it," Daarshan said. "The mountain is mostly made of it."

"So it makes the most sense to use it for the houses."

Daarshan's brother was looking at them with a puzzled expression on his face.

"What else would you use?" he said.

"We have wooden shingles or clay tiles in Ruph," Cat said.

"Wood?" He wrinkled his forehead, then he laughed. "Oh, you're having me on. You couldn't use wood on roofs, it's much too flimsy!"

"It's true," Daarshan put in. "They have wooden roofs there."

"Yeah, sure they do, Tiny," Jarin said with a smirk. "Hey, Tiny, guess what?" He slapped the door jamb of a house they were passing. "Aruna Nettersdaughter is apprenticing to Blaec Fisher!"

"Oh, is she?" Daarshan replied. "Doesn't surprise me."

It had been like that the whole way down from the mountain. Jarin had been rattling off the local news to Daarshan, tossing name after name at him—but not one question about where his brother had been, why he was back, how he'd been doing, let alone what the world was like outside this little town. And Daarshan reacted to it as if this was normal. The brothers obviously liked each other—even the names Jarin called Daarshan sounded more affectionate than insulting—but the relationship seemed to be all about the older brother.

They had reached the edge of the marketplace, and Guy pulled up the cart, then turned to the two young men.

"Where is the inn?"

"Over there," Daarshan said, pointing to a sizable building on the left, but at the same time Jarin said, "Oh, but

145

you must come to Father's house first! Come, come, this way!" He took the horse's bridle and pulled it to the right, towards the big house Daarshan had pointed out to them from the mountain.

Guy and Cat exchanged a glance, then Cat shrugged. Why not? Might as well meet these people now; there *were* Daarshan's family.

The house was enormous. Cat tipped back her head, looking up the wide two-story facade that dominated the whole side of the marketplace. Its overly elaborate slate siding, patterned in swirls, diamonds, chevrons, diagonals, loops, and garlands that were running from the eaves right down to the cobbles of the marketplace, set off the bright colours of the banner fluttering on the square little bell turret, gilded by the late-afternoon sun. What was that emblem in the centre of the flag—a silver-coloured goblet? Ah yes, of course, Daarshan's father was a silversmith, and apparently not one to hide his light under a bushel. Cat's eye travelled down the front of the house to a large bay window set into the left side of the facade, sparkling with silver goods on the display shelf behind it, and across a wide set of three stairs with an ornate railing that led up to a large door immediately to the right of the window, a prominent tradesman's sign hanging over top of it proclaiming that this was the entrance to the shop. Further to the right, a smaller, less ostentatious door, with a single step in front of it, looked like it might open onto the living quarters.

Jarin stopped the horse in front of the house.

"I'll take the cart around back," he said. "Take them inside, Squirt—Mother is going to have a fit when she sees you!"

Cat could see a muscle in Daarshan's cheek jump as he clenched his jaw. She lifted Yaya off the cart.

"Is this a good time to just drop in?" she said.

"Oh, sure, sure," Jarin replied, "just go on in!" He pointed to the smaller door. "Go on, Shrimp, what are you waiting for?"

Daarshan took a deep breath, then looked at Cat and Guy almost apologetically.

"Come, please," he said, and pushed the door open.

CHAPTER 21

JAMIE STEPPED INTO THE house behind Cat and Guy and the kids, kicking his heel out at the goat, which was trying to follow, and closing the door in its face. A tall woman stood by the window of the room they walked into from the hallway; she was greyish-blonde and had her hair wrapped around her head in that braided Princess-Leia style, the one from *The Return of the Jedi*, that a lot of the women in this world seemed to like.

If Daar's brother thought she was going to have a fit on seeing her younger son, he obviously didn't know his mother very well—unless a startled look and an "Oh!" constituted a fit in his books. In fact, Jamie would have doubted she *was* their mother, if it hadn't been for her blue eyes, which both her sons seemed to have inherited. If Jamie's mom saw him unexpectedly after being away for three weeks, she'd be all over him, hug him, ask a million questions about how he was doing and what he'd been up to, and not catch her breath for at least ten minutes. (Jamie felt a little stab at the thought. Would he actually ever see Mom again?)

But this lady was a total icicle. Actually, she almost looked like she was scared. Weird.

After a half a minute or so of staring at Daar, she seemed to thaw out a bit.

"How are you, son?"

Daar gave a little half-bow. Really? If he bowed to that lady, maybe she wasn't his mom after all, even though she called him 'son'. They addressed most younger guys that way here; Guy said it all the time. Maybe she was his aunt.

"I'm well, Mother," Daar said. (There went that theory.) "I've come from Ruph—"

Now that woke her up. "Ruph?" She looked from Daar to Cat and then to Guy, and something sparked in her eyes as if she recognised him. "Master Salmor Septimus?" she asked.

Guy smiled and bowed. "His son," he said. "Dyniselm Potter, called Guy, at your service."

The woman laughed at that. "Of course!" she said. "I was not thinking clearly, he would be much older now. You look much like he did when I left Ruph—more than thirty years now..." She gave her head a quick shake, as if she was brushing off a fly. "The Year of the Drought, that was. And of course, my Cousin Kaltbur's wife Yeryl is your sister, is she not?"

"That's so," Guy said. He gestured at the rest of them. "My wife Catriona, my children." His hand wave seemed to include Jamie in that description.

"I'm so pleased to meet you," Cat said, holding out her hand. "Come shake hands with Mistress Drabet, kids."

She was doing it again—making the Ginny kid shake hands with strangers. And sure enough, as soon as the kid's hand made contact with that of Daar's mother, she got that look on her face like she'd touched a live wire. This time her eyes got even bigger than when she'd shaken hands with Daar, back in Ruph when they first met. What was it with that family? Did they have really clammy hands or something? But then Jamie remembered what the kid had said—about being able to feel other people. She was some kind of clairvoyant. Maybe shaking their hands triggered it.

Before Jamie had a chance to shake hands with Mrs Daar's-Mother himself, the door opened again and the brother bounced into the room. The guy seemed like a bit of a jock—nice enough though, as far as that went.

"I put your goat in the courtyard with the horse," he announced. "Whatever did you bring a goat for?" Then, without waiting for an answer, he turned to his mother. "There, Mother, aren't you pleased Tiny is back?" He gave Daar a punch on the arm.

The mother looked at Jarin like he was the most amazing thing ever. "But yes, love, such a surprise," she said with a smile way brighter than what she'd given Daar himself when he walked in. There was a definite resemblance between those two. Daar looked nothing like either of them, aside from their eyes.

"I made them come here, because they wanted to see Father," Jarin said and rubbed the side of his nose. He looked around the room. "Where is Father? I need to tell him about Elil Fisher; his rudder broke and he needed me there to fix it."

"Ah, so you repair things too?" Guy put in.

"Oh, no," Jarin said. "The people just want me there while they do the work. It helps them. It's because I'm..."

"...the seventh son of the seventh son," a male voice interrupted. Jamie looked around. A man stepped into the room. He was on the short side, and his curly salt-and-pepper hair had obviously once been as dark as Daar's—in fact, he was the exact image of what Daarshan would look like in another forty years or so.

"Well done, son," he said to Jarin, patting him on the shoulder, "Elil ought to be pleased. I hope you told him a peck of mackerel from his next catch wouldn't come amiss."

Jarin looked a little sheepish. "Elil had a poor catch for the last few runs," he said. "I didn't like to ask. Besides, with his wife's bad leg—they've had it hard of late. He'll make it up to us somehow, I'm sure. But Father, haven't you seen—" He reached over and grabbed Daar by the arm, pulling him out from behind Guy, where he'd been half hidden.

The old guy got a deadpan look on his face. "Oh!" he said. Daar's parents sure were wordy in their greetings.

Daar gave that funny little half-bow again. "Father," he said, his voice sounding like he had a frog in his throat. His face had gone quite red, and he was fidgeting with a silver fork he'd picked up from the sideboard.

His father frowned. "Why are you back? Your cousin did not want to be saddled with you? I would have expected

151

even you could make yourself useful in some way some-where!"

"No, Father, I..." Daar stuttered, his face looking like a tomato. Suddenly there was a small metallic twanging noise, and he looked down at the fork in his hand. Now it looked like Uri Geller had been at it—bent backwards, the tines pointing in three different directions. Daar's face went chalk white.

The old man made a weird *Pshaw!* noise. "Just as clumsy as ever!" he growled. "It's no wonder you're of no use to anyone!" He grabbed the Frankenfork out of Daar's hand and waved it at him. "Just at solstice I made this set! It's anyone's guess if I'll be able to mend this!" He tossed it on the table with a clatter, then made another *Harumph!* noise.

Apparently even Jarin had caught on that their family reunion wasn't going as swimmingly as he'd expected, and he tried to turn the subject.

"Oh, Father, these are our cousins!" he said, waving his hand at the lot of them. "They've come to, uh—"

Guy took a step forward and put his hand on Daar's shoulder.

"Master Waldan," he said, nodding his head at the old guy in a brief greeting, "Guy Potter at your service." Then he gave the man an arrow-straight look. "I've come to discuss the terms of your son's apprenticeship."

CHAPTER 22

C AT PUT THEIR TRAVEL bag on the wide four-poster bed in the inn's bedroom and unstrapped the buckles. She looked across at Guy, who was sitting on the other side of the bed, pulling off his boots.

"The look on Waldan's face when you dropped that bomb on him was priceless," she said. "Well done, dear."

He grinned.

"I had to wipe that scowl off the man's face somehow," he said. "He's making my blood boil with the way he steps on that boy. I almost thought Daarshan was going to give it away, though; he looked as shocked as his father."

"Well, this *was* the first time he ever heard of an apprenticeship," said Cat, digging their nightshirts out of the bag and tucking them under the pillows. "Or any of us ever heard of it, for that matter. Jarin was the only one who looked pleased. He seems like a nice enough fellow, even if he's not the sharpest knife in the drawer—about the only one in Daarshan's family who likes him, by the looks of it. I don't think Daarshan knows what to make of it, to tell you the truth."

"Of the apprenticeship, you mean? Do you think he won't want to apprentice to me?"

"As to that, I don't know—but I think he doesn't know if you're serious or not." Cat walked around the bed to the other side of the room and squeezed herself into the narrow space between Guy's knees and the outer wall. She turned the wrought-iron handle of the small-paned window and pushed it open, looking down onto the market square bathed in the early-evening light.

"Well, I *am* serious," Guy said. "This might solve more problems than one. What do you think, Karana?"

"I think it's an excellent idea," Cat said. She leaned her elbows on the windowsill and took a deep breath of the tangy air that wafted in from the sea. "Ah, I love the ocean. And the view is gorgeous!"

"Mmm, it certainly is," said Guy from behind her.

Cat looked over her shoulder at him sitting on the bed. "How can you see anything? You'd have to look past my—"

He grabbed her around the waist and pulled her backwards onto the bed with him. "Did I say it was the view of the *ocean* I appreciated?"

"You—" She wiggled around and tried to smack him, but he caught her wrists and rolled over onto her.

"Now, now," he chided, "no such violence, my sweet!"

She pulled her hands free, caught his head and pulled it down to her for a kiss—a long, hard kiss that got deeper, and more intense, and...

A tremendous racket erupted outside the open window.

"Mumma, Mumma!"

"Maaaaaah!"

"Papa, the goat's got my..."

"Jamie, it's going that way!"

"Maaaaah!"

"Catch it!"

"Maaaaah!"

—ele—

"Goat stew!" Guy muttered vindictively, once Cory's coat was rescued, the goat securely penned in the inn's stable, and peace restored to their circle. "It had to interrupt us just when..."

"Shh," Cat hissed, "the kids!"

"Interrupt what, Mumma?" Cory said.

"Oh, nothing," Cat said, feeling her cheeks get a little warm.

"They were probably kissing," Bina said in a world-ly-wise tone.

"Kissing? Eeww!" Cory made a face.

"That was nothing, eh?" Guy murmured in Cat's ear from behind her and pinched her bottom.

She jumped and swatted his hand away, and out of the corner of her eye saw Jamie look pointedly the other way. A giggle formed in the back of her throat, and she gave Guy a mock glare over her shoulder. "Behave yourself," she whispered, "at least in public!"

"Mumma, I'm hungry," Cory said. "What are we having for supper?"

Guy secretly gave Cat another pinch. "Yes, what are we having for supper?"

She tried to stare him down. "If you don't stop that, you're going to bed *without* supper!" Then she realized what she had just said, and felt her face catch on fire.

Guy waggled his eyebrows. "Right now?"

"Cut it out!" she said, trying to keep a straight face. "And I don't know what we're having for supper. I think there's still some food left in our bag."

Daarshan came out of the inn's stable yard. Apparently he had overheard the last sentence; he looked a little embarrassed. "My mother said you are invited for dinner tomorrow, but she was not prepared for guests tonight."

"Of course not!" Cat said. "We didn't expect her to feed us—putting food on the table for seven extra bodies is no small feat. Don't worry, we'll find something."

"What's this over there?" Bina asked, pointing to a small shop tucked between a netter's and a butcher's on the side of the square. The shop sign advertised "Fish Rolls", and a couple of people sat at a table in front of the shop, eating something from wraps of paper. "Do they sell food?"

"Oh, yes," Daarshan said. "It's a special dish we make here. I like it a lot."

"That sounds good," said Guy, whose hand was resting on the middle of Cat's back, "let's try it."

Guy and Jamie had to duck so as not to hit their heads on the low ceiling beams inside the little shop. Chairs and small tables were scattered in the front part of the room, and a dark-skinned woman with a round face stood behind the counter across the back end, dishing something onto plates. She nodded a greeting at them.

They settled the kids around two of the tables, and Guy went with Daarshan to the counter to get the food.

"So what is this then?" Guy asked as they came back carrying half a dozen plates covered with napkins.

"It's fish wrapped in rice with vinegar and seaweed," Daarshan replied.

"What?" cried Cat. "That sounds like—" She pulled one of the napkins off the plate. "It is! It's sushi!"

"Oh, great," said Jamie, "I love sushi."

"Sushi?" Guy asked with a raise of his eyebrows.

"It's from my—our—my old world," Cat said, picking up one of the little black-and-white pinwheels. "I used to buy this for my lunches when I was working at the library in Greenward Falls!" She took a bite and closed her eyes in bliss as the familiar salty and tangy flavour filled her mouth. "It tastes almost exactly like the kind I used to get," she said. "No pickled ginger or soy sauce, though."

"Do you want pickles with it?" Daarshan asked. "They have those too." He went to the counter and came back with a jar of red relish.

"This looks different than what I'm used to," said Cat, "but that's okay. It smells great." She dished out some of the pink pickle, which turned out to be a concoction mostly of beets, and found it quite an acceptable condiment to accompany the sushi—or fish rolls, as it were.

She was half done her plate when she heard the shop door open behind her. Daarshan, across the table from her, looked up.

"Ah, Mistress Cat," he said, "you wanted to meet him."

Cat turned around. A middle-aged man had entered the shop. He was tall and broad-shouldered, with dark hair that had white streaks along the temples and waved back from the point of a strong widow's peak. His warm brown eyes looked at them questioningly, then they fell on Daarshan, and he raised his eyebrows in recognition.

"You're back then, Silversmithson?"

Daarshan was on his feet now and gave one of his little bows.

"Master Coshy, this is Mistress Catriona. She—she is a bookwoman, and has come especially from—from Ruph to meet you."

Cat jumped up. Coshy! Coshy the Poet, finally!

"I'm so very pleased to make your acquaintance, Master Coshy." She held out her hand.

Coshy rubbed a finger along the side of his nose, then stretched out his hand and took hers with quite a charming smile.

"All the way from Ruph, and a bookwoman? We must talk. I have no leisure tonight, but come to my house in the morning. The boy will show you." He pointed his chin at Daarshan. "I must go now, but we will speak tomorrow." He went to the counter and picked up a small wooden box. "My supper," he said, gesturing with the box. "Give my regards to your mother, Silversmithson." He walked out the door with a nod goodbye.

Cat was in awe. She had just met her favourite poet! And she was invited to his house to talk with him! She felt a little star-struck—maybe that was why she had this vague feeling that she had met this man somewhere before?

CHAPTER 23

*D*EAR ANDY, COSHY NETTER *is letting me have paper and ink to write to you while he and Mum are talking about poetry and books. Papa and Mum and Yaya and me are staying at the Inn, and the boys are all sleeping at Daar's* ~~house~~ *parents' house. Me and Yaya have a tiny little room to ourselves, next to the one Mum and Papa have, and we have a window that looks out at the sea.*

Andy, I ~~love~~ LOVE *the sea! Daar took us to his favourite beach, on the other side of town away from the harbour. Is the ocean that beautiful in Rhanathon, too? So big, and blue, and sparkly. Before we came, Mum told us that the sea was like the lake at home, the one that we go swimming in sometimes in summer, but it's not. It's much, much, much more. It's so oceanish! I love the sound the water makes as it rushes up to the shore, and the shells, and the crabs (the hermit crabs! I want to bring one home, but Mum says it wouldn't be happy without the ocean and a new shell to move into when it gets bigger, and we don't have those at home). And getting your toes in the sand, and the funny stuff that's called sea onions.*

Do you have those on the beach in Rhanathon? They look like real onions, like a bulb, but they're hollow, with a long brown slimy tail. Cory picked one up by its tail and swung it around, and it hit Daar, and it went "fthup". Daar was really surprised at first, but then he laughed and picked one up too, and tried to hit Cory back, but he got Jamie instead, so then Jamie got him with one, but Papa got in the way and Jamie hit him in the face with the sea onion bulb. And both him and Daar were scared for a minute, because they were afraid that Papa would be mad at them. But Papa laughed and grabbed a sea onion too, and he whacked Jamie back much harder, and then they were all whacking each other with the sea onions and laughing so hard they could barely stand up. And then Jamie slipped and landed on his bum in the water, and they all laughed even more until he splashed Papa, who was laughing the hardest at him, and then we all ended up in the water and splashed each other like mad.

I don't think Daar's ever had fun with a grown-up like that before. He felt really happy, but underneath he was surprised about it and not sure what to think. ~~I don't think his father likes~~ I can't talk about it here, because I'm writing this in ~~Cosby's~~ someone else's house and I don't know how they send their mail here and if somebody is going to read it. But Andy, Daar's family ~~is doesnt has a secret~~ is so different from ours. Nobody at home thinks Papa is all that special because of being the Septimissimus, but here they think Daar's brother Jarin, who's a Septimus, is the most amazing thing ever. Specially his father, he's so proud of him, but doesn't care about Daar. And his mother too, but she's got a different reason (I can't tell you right now) (I don't know if Daar knows). I wish you were here so I could ask you what to do.

Yaya wants to go to the beach and find more seashells and play with the crabs right now, so I'm going to take him so Mum can keep talking with Coshy. The guys and Papa are all at Cinda Potter's, she's the great-great-granddaughter of the potter Daar told us about who could hunt with his bare hands. Papa wants to get her glaze recipe for that sand they have on the beach here (it's blue in some places). He'll send you the recipe if it turns out. I've got to go, but I'll tell you more about Arkaroth later.

Love, Bina

PS: Sorry about the ink blots, Yaya made me spill.

CHAPTER 24

"IT'S BEEN A PLEASURE talking with you, Mistress." Coshy Netter held out his hand to Cat. "How long will you be staying in town?"

Cat took the offered hand. "We're not quite sure yet," she said. "A couple of days, probably. We're going to dinner at the Silvermith's house today, then we'll see."

"Ah! The Silversmith's." Coshy rubbed a finger along the side of his nose. "Good food, that's what Drabet makes. The company, however... Good food, I say." He laughed. "Well, if you find yourself with another few minutes to spare before you take your leave, come on by again for another chinwag. I don't get much chance to talk with another lover of literature."

"I'll try," Cat said.

She had very much enjoyed her visit with the poet. The two hours they had spent together had flown by in a discussion of the authors he had on his shelf, the books that had come out recently in the big cities, verse structure and the process of writing...

Cat had been particularly interested to hear how Coshy wrote his poems. Apparently he thought up most of his verse while he did his work, sitting at the netting loom. As the fishing net grew knot by knot, he said, his poems tied themselves together in his mind. Then all he had to do was write them down.

"Quiet work done with one's hands, tied to the earth," he'd said, "leaves the mind free to soar, like the gulls out over the harbour. There's many a catch of our fishermen that was snared in the knots of my verse." He'd laughed at that, as he did at many of his pronouncements.

Cat smiled as she walked down the narrow street from Coshy's house towards the market. The poet was quite different from what she had assumed—not at all the brooding artist that studying Byron and Shelley in college had taught her to expect. He was a working man, cheerful and good-natured, with a genuine interest in his fellow men. But it was this very interest in others, Cat thought, that led to his poetry being what it was, that synthesis of observations of the human experience and the natural world that made his verses so appealing. Cat slipped her hand into her satchel and ran her fingers over the smooth leather cover of the book he'd given her, a copy of his latest volume. She very much looked forward to reading it. He had read her the first few poems out loud; she would always hear them in his voice after this.

"An orange ball of flame
Sinks to the sea.
Drowning
Itself

To rise ablaze

To newborn day…"

"I'd thought of calling that one 'Self-Sacrifice'," Coshy had said, "but then I just went with 'Sunset'. The good people hereabouts don't go in for too much double meaning, and it doesn't do to shatter their illusions." He'd laughed, then dipped his pen in the inkwell and with a flourish signed the flyleaf of Cat's book.

He hadn't been wrong about the food that Drabet had prepared, either. The table in the Silversmith's dining room was loaded with an impressive spread, in enormous quantities. Soup, meat, potatoes, rice, about four different vegetable dishes, and small round seed-studded buns to wipe up the sauces made up the main course, while for dessert there was a selection of candied fruits, puddings, and nuts, including something that was an awful lot like coconut, bought straight off some fishing boats from across the Moon Sea. It was all delicious, but Cat was so stuffed she couldn't eat more than a piece or two of fruit for dessert.

"Can I help with clearing up?" she asked Drabet.

"No, thank you," the Silversmith's wife said, bustling out into the kitchen with another empty dish.

Cat wasn't surprised at Drabet's refusal. She wasn't a very sociable person, this mother of Daarshan's, and neither were the few of her older children Cat had met. One of the sons, a journeyman toolsmith, came by to deliver an order of silversmithing tools to his father, stayed for a quick bite to eat, and then went back to work, while the two daughters, who had come to help their mother with the food, only sat down at the table long enough to eat a little and then were back in the kitchen.

All of them were in their late twenties and married; the older daughter had brought her own two little girls, who kept Yaya entertained by treating him as a live doll. The children got to eat in the kitchen, which Cat was glad for—Coshy had not been wrong about the adult company, either, and Cat was happy to spare Bina the tension at Waldan's table.

Jarin was the only pleasant person in that family, as far as Cat was concerned—cheerful and friendly, he seemed genuinely happy to have his brother back in town. He was also the only one who got much of a reaction out of Drabet. She obviously doted on her second-youngest—with smiles, kind words, extra tidbits on his plate, small caresses—nothing that would be at all remarkable in the interaction between mother and child, were it not for the complete absence of similar signs of affection with any of her other children.

And her behaviour towards Daarshan was downright puzzling. It was almost as if she did not want him in the house, wanted to keep him away from his father, and the few glances Cat caught her throwing at her youngest son seemed to have an undertone of fear.

Daarshan sat at the far end of the table, poking at his food with his eyes lowered. The Silversmith ignored him for the most part, except for the odd frown and a criticism or two—the boy was slouching; he held his spoon wrong; he had a spot on the collar of his shirt...

The comments made Daarshan increasingly clumsy. Almost as soon as Waldan had drawn attention to the stain on the shirt, it was joined by another, and as for the offending spoon, it dropped right out of Daarshan's fingers, leading to his fishing around for it under the table, emerging scarlet-faced, stammering an apology, then bumping his elbow into his cup.

Guy, who sat across the table from Daarshan, lunged to catch the cup in the nick of time to save it from spilling, and he set it upright again with a little more force than was strictly necessary. There was a frown line forming between his eyebrows, so subtle only Cat knew it was there, as he looked at Waldan.

At the moment the man was bragging about his seventh son's popularity in the town. Jarin, who sat at his father's right hand side, was obviously Waldan's pride and joy, and he drew him into the limelight at every opportunity, encouraging him to talk of his work in the town, and boasting of his Septimus gift.

This gift, from what Cat could gather, consisted of boosting the ability of the town's inhabitants to get their work done more effectively. Cat was not surprised—one part of Guy's Septimissimus gift manifested in a similar way, by strengthening others' abilities. But Guy only used it sparingly, where it was needful, while Jarin seemed to see this as his chief task and spent the bulk of his days moving around the town, finding opportunities to assist the townsfolk while they worked. He appeared to do it out of a genuine desire to be a help to his neighbours—another point that made Cat disposed to like the young man.

Waldan, on the other hand, seemed to be less concerned with the good of the villagers than with what his son's gift could garner him and his family.

"He won't even ask for payment from the fisherfolk," he said to Guy, spearing a honey-coated peach on his silver fork. "You need to be more forceful, my boy,"—he jabbed the peach in Jarin's direction—"else they will take advantage of us!" With a little plop, he dunked the fruit into his pudding bowl, then stuffed it into his mouth.

"They won't take advantage, Father," Jarin said with a little chuckle. He smiled over his shoulder at his mother, who had just laid three more pieces of candied fruit on his plate. Her fingers stroked the nape of his neck, her whole face suffused with loving warmth for a moment as she met his eyes. Jarin picked up a slice of pear and took a bite. "Mmh, delicious, Mother," he said. "The people do what they can, Father," he continued, popping the rest of the pear into his mouth and swallowing, "there's no need to ask."

"Hah, that's what you think, son!" Waldan waved another impaled peach around as he gestured with his fork. "You need to be on your toes, look out for our interests. With a gift like yours..."

"With a gift like mine, Father, I have to serve the people," Jarin replied good-naturedly, reaching for the silver cruet stand in the middle of the table and sprinkling some of the white coconut-like flakes from one of its three dishes onto his pudding. Cat got the feeling that this was not the first time they'd had this argument, but she nevertheless found it awkward to have to listen to it.

Jarin took some nuts from the cruet dish. "Hey Tiny," he said, "catch!" and he tossed them across the table at his brother. Daarshan, startled, flung up his hand to grab the nuts, but instead he knocked into his pudding dish, tipping it and sending the contents gushing onto the table cloth, while the nuts bounced off his forehead.

"*Pshaw*!" snorted Waldan. He gave Daarshan a withering glance, then tossed his napkin on the table and pushed back his chair.

"I have to get back to work," he said. "Leave your brother's mess, Jarin, the women will clean it up. Master Guy, I shall see you again before you leave town, I'm sure." He stalked out of the room.

Jarin, with a grin on his face, gave up trying to scoop Daarshan's pudding back into the bowl and handed over the spoon to his mother.

"Hey, you didn't eat your nuts, Shrimp," he said, picking up the small brown morsels from the tabletop where they had landed.

Daarshan, who was fiddling with the strings on his shirt collar, gave him a look. "I don't like nuts," he said. "Never have."

"Oh! Really? Don't know why, they're great," Jarin said. He tossed the nuts into his own mouth and crunched down on them. "So, what are you doing this afternoon? I'm going to help Calder Wheelwright, he's having some trouble with his lathe. I'd say come along, but I don't think it would be much good, I couldn't pay as much attention. And it's not like you'd be any help."

There was a small snapping sound as Daarshan's shirt collar strings broke.

CHAPTER 25

C AT STRETCHED LIKE HER namesake animal and swung her legs over the edge of the bed. What a treat to have a nice, leisurely nap in the middle of the day! Guy had taken Cory and Yaya off for another trip to the beach so she could have some time to herself. And after that meal at Drabet and Waldan's house, a nap was what she'd needed. The tension in that family was hard on the nerves, downright exhausting.

Cat pulled on her shoes. She'd go check on the goat in the pen in the inn's stable yard, and then maybe go across to the sushi place for another plate of fish rolls. She was ecstatic to have found that place—she hadn't realized how much she'd missed sushi until she'd tasted some again. They had rice in Ruph, but only sometimes—it was hideously expensive, because it had to be imported from across the Moon Sea and then transported by cart into the mountains. But here at the coast, they got it straight from the source, via fishing boats that came from Asbanar and brought rice for trading. As for the seaweed for wrapping the rolls, they harvested and dried it themselves, the little shop's proprietor had told her. Cat wondered how hard it would be to make sushi herself, if she brought a supply of seaweed and rice home with her.

She was about to pull open the door on the little side shed in the stable yard when she heard a noise. A crash, like breaking crockery, and then a shout and laughter. That sounded like Bina! And was that Jamie and Daarshan? Cat followed the sound.

Behind the stables, in the corner by the inn's waste dump, the three young people were gathered around a small wooden crate that seemed to be full of misshapen and cracked pottery, some glazed and other pieces still raw—obviously a potter's crackpot bin, like the one Guy had in his workshop, where he tossed the pieces that had warped or broken in the kiln.

"Okay, try it again!" Bina said.

With a shrug, Daarshan took a piece of pottery out of the bin—an unglazed jug without a handle.

"My turn," Bina said. She gave Daarshan a measuring look, from head to toe and back up again. "You look like you slept in your clothes last night," she said, "and your hair looks like a bird's nest!"

There was a flash of annoyance in the boy's eyes, and the jug in his hands cracked in half.

"Yes!" "Hah!" Bina and Jamie shouted, and Daarshan gave a reluctant grin. He dropped the broken pieces onto the inn's waste pile, then took out of the bin a little bowl whose glaze had crawled badly, patches of the dish bare.

"It's not really true," Bina said, "I only said that, about your clothes and hair, I mean."

Jamie scoffed. "Uh-huh," he said, "sure! My grandma's dog's shag is tidier than Frodo's head! He probably doesn't even know what a comb looks like!"

The dish shattered in Daarshan's hands.

"All right!" Jamie yelled, and he raised his hand for a high-five.

The scowl on Daarshan's face cleared, and the boys slapped their palms together.

"I think you're right, kid," Jamie said to Bina. "When Frodo gets mad, he breaks things."

"My name's not Frodo," Daarshan said.

"Wait, wait," Bina said, "take another one, and then think about that!"

He fished a cracked mug out of the bin.

"Frodo," said Jamie in a taunting sing-song, "Frodo, Frodo, Frodo!"

The little mug blew apart with a loud crack, and they shouted with triumph.

"That was a good one," Bina said. "It's not only when you're mad, though, is it? It's other kinds of upset, too."

Daarshan took another chipped mug out of the box, and ran his thumbs over the rough surface. "I don't know," he said, "it just happens. I can't help it."

"Huh, you're probably just not trying," Jamie said.

Daarshan's eyebrows drew down into a frown. "I am! But it just ha-"

Crack! The mug shattered with such force a piece of it hit Jamie in the face.

"Ow!" He clapped a hand to his cheek. "Watch it there, Frodo!"

Bina laughed. "Serves you right," she said, "you provoked him!"

"That was the idea, wasn't it—*Frodo*?" Jamie rubbed at his cheek, smearing blood from the small cut on his cheek bone down his jawline.

Daarshan had picked a misshapen bowl out of the bin and was cupping his hands around it.

"You can't get to me," he said. "My brother calls me names, and it doesn't bother me. He calls me Tiny, and Shrimp, and Shorty, and Squirt, and..."

There was a small snapping sound, and a crack ran down the bowl.

"Oh yeah," Jamie said, "that doesn't bother you? Sure, that's why that thing is breaking up in your hands! Your family can call you names, and you—"

Daarshan's eyes narrowed. "You know nothing about my family," he said. "You know nothing about my life! You know nothing about anything!" *Crack!* The shards of the bowl flew in all directions, and Daarshan scooped another one out of the bin, scowling fiercely. "Why don't you go back to where you came from? Oh yes, because you don't know how, that's why! You don't know *anything*!" *Crack!* The splinters went flying, and he snatched up a mug without a handle, weighing it in his hand like a missile. "You don't have a clue, do you? You'll probably be stuck here forever, because..." *Crack!* Almost before the pieces hit the ground, another pot was in his hands.

Jamie's face now wore a scowl to match Daarshan's. "Well, *Frodo*, at least I don't have a mom who totally freezes me out—"

CRACK! Daarshan's face twisted into a grimace of fury, and he snatched a heavy, warped teapot out of the bin.

"—and a dad who treats me like a piece of scum!"

CRACK! The pot exploded. For a split second Daarshan stared at the broken handle left in his hand, his face frozen into a mask of anger and pain. Then he hauled back and flung the piece at Jamie. It missed his head by a fraction of an inch. For a moment the two boys glared at each other, chests heaving—and with a snarl, Daarshan lunged at Jamie.

This had gone too far! Cat started forward, but all of a sudden there was Guy beside her with his hand on her arm, holding her back.

"Leave them," he said, "they need this."

Bina stood on the side with her eyes wide, her knuckles in her mouth, as the boys punched, hit, shoved, and smacked each other—one moment Daarshan had Jamie on the ground, giving him a punch to the head, the next Jamie sat astride Daarshan, pushing his face into the dirt, then Daarshan fought to the top and got Jamie in a headlock, pummelling his chest. Grunting, yelling, struggling, fists flying—then Daarshan was sitting on Jamie's chest, his fingers dug into his shoulders, and he was shaking him, his teeth clenched, pounding Jamie against the ground with heaving, sobbing breaths.

"Enough now." Guy stepped over, got his arm around Daarshan's chest and hauled him back. "Enough, son." He pulled the boy off Jamie, then reached out a hand, clasped Jamie's and drew him to his feet. "You've made your point, both of you."

Daarshan dragged his fist across his nose, smearing blood across his face, and he drew a shuddering breath. His clothes hung in tatters—the fabric was shredded, and it looked as if every seam had ripped; dark bruises were starting to show through the holes in his shirt. Jamie didn't look much better—his clothes weren't quite shredded, but dirty and torn, and he was developing a beautiful black eye. He rubbed his shoulders where Daarshan had gripped him.

"Holy moley!" Cory's voice came from behind Cat. "What happened to you guys?"

"They had a fight," Cat said. "Where's Yaya?"

"Aw man," Cory complained, "I miss all the best stuff! Yaya's having a nap, Mumma. Hey, Daar, your underwear is showing."

Daarshan looked down on himself and blushed crimson when he saw that his shredded pants were exposing his linen underbreeches—and with another ripping sound, even those weren't providing much coverage any more.

With a smirk, Guy whipped off his coat and tossed it to the boy. "Cover up, son, you don't want to frighten the ladies. And here,"—he pulled a handkerchief out of his pocket—"hold that to your nose. I don't want you bleeding all over my coat." Then he put his hand on the boy's shoulder, and looked across at Cat. "I think a clean-up is in order, don't you? There's a bath in the inn. After getting this close-up and personal, you boys might as well share it between you." He quirked up an eyebrow at Jamie.

"Yes," Cat said. "Daarshan, you need a change of clothes. But you won't want to go back to your parents' house in this state."

The look in the boy's blue eyes told her she was right.

"Cory can get them," Bina put in, "can't he?"

Daarshan looked relieved and nodded. He was awkwardly clutching Guy's coat around his waist with one hand and pressing Guy's handkerchief to his nose with the other, the square of fabric already soaked through with blood. "Dey're in by bag," he said, "by clodes, I bean. In de room."

"Okay, got it!" Cory ran off.

"Here," Bina said. She picked a couple of large fuzzy leaves off a grey-green plant that grew at the bottom of the stable wall and held them out to Daarshan. "It's flannel plant—stick it up your nose, it'll help."

He lowered the handkerchief, releasing another gush of blood, and took the leaves from Bina, scrunching them up and pushing them into his nostrils. The lower half of his face was covered in blood; he was smeared with dirt, had a cut on his brow, and the leaves stuffed up his nostrils looked like some bizarre growth sprouting from his nose.

Jamie, whose shiner was darkening by the minute, gave him a look. Daarshan stared back at him, deadpan, for a few heartbeats. Then Jamie's mouth began to twitch. Daarshan gave a little grunt, then a snort—and they both burst out laughing, a howling, thigh-slapping, doubling-over paroxysm that pulled Cat, Guy and Bina right along with it.

"All right," Guy said, when they could finally catch their breath, "you two are coming with me. The bath is this way." He gripped each of the boys by a shoulder and steered them towards the back door of the inn.

"Hey, Fr—Daar," Cat heard Jamie say as they walked away, "first dibs on the tub!"

She looked at Bina with a raise of her eyebrows. "This whole thing was your idea, wasn't it?" she said. "You're lucky a bloody nose and a black eye are all that came of this, missie."

Bina twisted her mouth sideways and tipped her head, then she shrugged. "No, I knew it was going to be fine," she said. "Daar didn't know it was his feelings that make things break in his hands. Now that he knows, it'll be okay. And punching Jamie helped him feel better, too."

Cat laughed. "You're ruthless! Did you know that that's where this was going to end?"

"Nope," Bina said, using her foot to shove the broken pottery pieces into a heap towards the garbage pile. "But it worked. Can you help me take Cinda Potter's bin back to her?"

"All right, puppet mistress," said Cat. "But this isn't all, is it? There's something else you're feeling, something about Daarshan. I can't tell what it is, but I know you do."

"Uh-huh," the girl said. Her expression grew serious. "It's about his mother and his father. And his brother. I don't really know what to do." She picked up one end of the crackpot bin.

"That's where I thought the issue was, too," Cat said, lifting the other end of the box. "Come on. Why don't you tell me about it, and we'll figure it out together."

CHAPTER 26

T HERE WASN'T A PROPER path up into the woods
where Daarshan was leading them to find the blue
rocks for Jamie's travel bowls. Once they had left the road
a few hundred yards above the last houses, they had struck
out straight into the forest, and they were now weaving
through the trees and underbrush, climbing higher and
higher on the hillside behind the town.

"How do you know where to go?" Cory asked, huffing
behind Daarshan who was carrying Yaya piggyback.

"I've come here often enough," Daarshan said. "I found
it one day when I was a kid; I don't think a lot of other
people know about it."

He'd probably spent a lot of time by himself as a child,
Cat thought. Yet another thing courtesy of a family who
lavished all their attention on the special seventh son
and had no time to spare for an unwanted eighth. Being
around Daarshan's parents really made her appreciate her
in-laws, who hadn't played favourites among their children, even though one of them was twice as special as a
"mere" seventh son.

"You can hardly hear the sea any more from here," Bina said, skirting around a prickly bush that looked like an Oregon grape.

"The trees muffle it," Jamie said from the back of the line. "I guess you have to see the sea to hear it, see?"

Cat looked around and grinned at him with a roll of her eyes at his pun. He grinned back, cheerfully slapping out a rhythm against the head of the small chisel-edged hammer in his belt, which he had borrowed from Daarshan's brother to hammer his rocks out of the hill.

"You'll see the ocean again in a minute," Daarshan said, "and hear it, too. We're almost there."

"Almos' dere, almos' dere!" Yaya sang, kicking his feet with the rhythm.

"Sweetie, stop kicking, Daarshan's not a horse!" Cat said.

Daarshan looked back and gave her a brief smile. "It's all right, Mistress Cat," he said, "I don't mind."

"Horsey, horsey!" Yaya cried, bouncing up and down and banging his heels into Daarshan's hips.

Guy laughed. "Wrong thing to say, Daarshan." With a few long strides, he made his way to the front of the line and lifted his youngest off Daarshan's back. "Cut it out, you little rascal," he said and swung the child onto his own shoulders. "Watch your head now." He grabbed Yaya by the hands, steadying him, and strode out behind Daarshan, who was turning the corner past a tall thicket.

Suddenly Guy stopped. "Wow!"

Cory came up behind him. "What is it, Papa—oh, wow!"

Cat followed them around the corner, and she caught her breath at the sight that met their eyes.

They had come out into a tiny natural quarry. On their right rose a blue-grey wall of rock some ten feet high, the layers of slate, like the uneven edges of a giant hand-cut book, forming the backdrop for the view that had opened up on their left, a wide vista of nothing but emerald tree-tops, gleaming indigo sea, and an endless expanse of azure sky. Far below them, they could hear the roaring of the surf; above in the sky, the raucous cry of the seagulls.

"Yeah, that's pretty wow all right," Jamie said with an appreciative look at the view. "And is this where you found the—"

"Maaaaah!" came a cry from behind them.

Cat whipped her head around. Unbelievable! How had the goat got there? She'd been sure it had been securely locked up in the inn's stable with the horse—but apparently not securely enough.

"Silly goat!" Bina said. She had it by the horns, trying to wrestle it aside, but it tossed its head, shook her off and bounded past her into the open space.

"Maaaaah!" With a few jumps, it scaled the quarry, looking down on them from the top edge of the rock wall with its slit-pupilled yellow eyes.

"And maaaaah to you, too!" Bina called after it. She turned to Daarshan. "So, Daar, is this your secret place? Where the blue rocks are? This is *glorious*!" She tipped back her head, drew in a deep breath of sea air, stretched out her arms, and twirled in a circle, her copper hair floating around her like a cape.

Daarshan's blue eyes were shining with the success of his surprise.

"Yes, this is where they are," he said. "It took me a while to find them; they're right—" He made his way over to the far edge, where the rock wall jutted out over a sharp drop-off. "They were right—" He looked up and down the wall, from side to side, then stepped close to the edge and ran his hand over a section of the rock. "I was sure—"

Guy went over and examined the rock wall. "What's this part?" he asked, tapping on a jagged chunk.

"I don't know," Daarshan said, his eyebrows drawing down into a frown. "I thought—I thought that's wher e..."

"Could the section with the blue rocks have cracked off? This looks like a freshly broken face."

Daarshan ran his thumb over the sharp slate edge. "I—I don't—" He leaned over and looked down the drop. "It—maybe—Ow!" A chunk of the slate cracked off and with a rumble dropped out of sight. Daarshan whipped back his thumb and clutched it in his other hand, hissing in air through his teeth. His eyes were narrowed in pain and frustration, and there was a deep crease between his eyebrows.

"Ouch, you cut yourself," Bina said. "But Daar, this isn't your fault! Papa, tell him."

Guy put his hand on the boy's shoulder and drew him away from the cliff edge.

"The blue rocks not being here?" he said. "Of course that's not your fault, son. Or did you come up here and hammer them off this morning?"

Daar raised his eyes to Guy, his face showing no response to Guy's mild joke.

"I—I'm so sorry," he said. "I—I thought they were here—I thought..."

Guy's hand tightened on his shoulder.

"I'll warrant they were," he said. "You could not have known they had broken off."

"Yeah," Jamie unexpectedly put in. "I mean, this totally sucks, but—" The disappointment he felt was clear on his face, but he struggled on. "I mean, it's not your damn—dang fault. I mean—shit." He picked up a piece of slate from the ground and threw it against the rock in frustration. Another chunk broke out of the wall.

"There," Guy said, "that's how easily it breaks." He gave Jamie a look that Cat knew was approval; the boy was trying hard.

Daar's frown had not let up. He dropped down onto a log that had fallen across the quarry floor and stared at the ground.

"I'm sorry," he mumbled again, "I thought—I wanted to help—" He picked up a piece of slate from the ground and started to worry it in his hands, oblivious to the cut on the ball of his thumb that was leaving a streak of blood on the rock.

Bina sat down beside him and put her hand over his. "Don't," she said. "Don't let them go into the rock. Your feelings, I mean. Just hold them for a minute and let them be. They're okay, you don't have to break the rock with them."

Cat gave her a surprised look. The girl had found exactly the right thing to say. But was Daarshan ready to hear it?

The boy gripped the rock so hard his knuckles turned white, and with a crack, it split in half. He hurled it to the ground and buried his head in his hands. "It's no good!" he said, brokenly. "It's just no good."

Cat crouched down in front of Daarshan and gently pulled his hand away from his face. "What's no good?" she said, wrapping her handkerchief around the cut thumb.

He turned his head away. "Me," he said in a low voice. "I'm no use."

Guy sat down on the log beside the boy. "What makes you think you're no good, son?"

Daarshan made a dispirited, scoffing noise and gestured at the broken slate piece and at the jagged edge of the rock wall.

"The fact that you break things?" Guy said. "I wonder."

Bina leaned forward to see past Daarshan, and she gave her father a bright-eyed, curious look. "What do you wonder, Papa?"

Guy turned his head and looked Daarshan in the face. "How long has this been going on, you breaking things, I mean?"

The boy raised his eyes to Guy's, then dropped them again. "I—I don't know. Two years or so, I think."

"Two years—so it started when you were, what, fourteen?"

Daarshan nodded.

"I thought as much," Guy said. "It seems to happen in groups of seven, every seventh birthday."

The boy glanced up with a puzzled frown, and Cat exchanged a look with Guy as she sat down on the log beside Bina. So he was onto the same thing she and Bina had already suspected?

"On my fourteenth birthday," Guy said, "my skills as an apprentice potter took a sudden jump. I got my journeymanship not long after. And it happened again on my twenty-first, so I had my mastership before I was twenty-two. And at twenty-eight,"—he looked across at Cat with a lopsided grin—"I started having holes in my pottery. Piece after piece, at least one in every firing. And I got horribly clumsy; I still have the scars to show for it."

"I didn't know that about your apprenticeship," Cat said. "But the holes, they stopped when you accepted who you really are—the seventh son of the seventh son. It's like your gift backfired until you knew it and embraced it."

Daarshan scowled at them from under his eyebrows. "I don't think my brother's ever had that problem," he said.

Bina laughed. "Not your brother, silly—you!"

He looked confused.

"We think," Cat said gently, "that it's really you who is your father's seventh son."

"What?!?"

"Jarin has a different father."

Daarshan's blue eyes widened until they were like saucers, and he went pale. "No!" he said. "No! It's Jarin who is the seventh son! It's him! He has to be! He's the one! He can't—I mean, how—who..."

"Who is his real father, if not Waldan? Think—might there be a possibility..." Guy said.

The boy's face flushed up, and he frantically shook his head. "No, no! No, it can't be! *No!*"

Bina tipped her head and laid her hand on his arm. "It's all right, Daar, it's okay! Papa..."

Guy put his hands on the boy's shoulders. "Steady on, son, steady on." He lightly rubbed Daarshan's shoulders, and the boy visibly calmed down.

"You know who it is, don't you?" Bina said.

Daarshan nodded reluctantly. "If—if this is true, then it has to—to be..."

"Coshy the Poet," Cat completed. Daarshan nodded again. "Bina felt it when she shook your mother's hand," Cat said. "Coshy is a close friend of your mother's, and I saw the resemblance between him and your brother—it's not obvious, but it's there. They have some of the same quirks, and the same hairline. And then there's your gift."

"What gift?"

"You can solve problems, son." Guy gave Daarshan's shoulders a squeeze. "Find solutions, fix things, like none I've known before."

"But that's not—that's... It's Jarin who has the gift!"

"His ability to help the people?" Cat said. "I admit, that had me stumped for a while, too. What do you think, dear?" She looked at Guy.

But it was Bina who answered. "Pla-Placebo Effect," she said. "They think him being there helps, and so it does. 'Cause he doesn't actually *do* anything, does he?" She looked at Daarshan.

He shook his head. "Not—not really. He's just there, and they can do their work better. It turns out better."

"Exactly," Bina said in a satisfied tone. "But *you* fix things, yourself. With your hands, or with knowing what to do."

"That's right," Cat said. "Like with Guy's glaze, you knew to put in vinegar to cut the lye. And you had the idea of putting Jamie's rocks in the travel glaze, and it worked."

Jamie, who stood off to the side, listening, nodded. "It's true, dude. There was that wheel on the cart on the way to Ruph that you fixed without knowing how to, too."

Daarshan looked up at him. "But—but I break things. I broke your bowl. And the stones here—they're—they're gone."

"That's not your fault!" Cat, Bina and Guy chorused together, which made them all laugh. Daarshan looked from one of them to the other, then he broke into a reluctant smile.

Cat smiled back at him. "Like Bina said earlier, Daarshan—it's your feelings that make you break things. I think it's a side effect of being gifted the way you, and Guy, are. His gift, when he didn't know it and wasn't using it right, made him ruin his pots and hurt himself; it looks like yours makes things explode in your hands."

Guy took his hands off Daarshan's shoulders and held them out in front of the boy. "See those?" he said, rubbing his thumb over some white scars on the backs of his fingers. "That's what I was talking about—permanent reminders of when I didn't know who or what I was. I don't recommend ignoring a Septimus gift." He gave Daarshan a light clap on the back. "So then, son, the question is what we do with that piece of knowledge. You're the seventh son of the seventh son. Do you want to announce it publicly and take your proper place in this town? You have every right to do so."

Cat watched the expressions chase each other over Daarshan's face. Hope, doubt, confusion, sadness, resignation, back to hope...

"We'd back you up," she said. "The word of the Septimissimus of Ruph surely would hold some weight, even here."

"That's right," Guy said. "I've no doubt that you really are the rightful Septimus. Your gifts bear you out. I've kept who I am under wraps here—didn't want people fawning over me and making a fuss. But I'd let it be known, to speak up for you."

"People?" Daarshan said, his tone bitter. "You mean my father."

Guy gave a rueful grin. "Yes, mostly. I thought he'd make a big deal of it, and I didn't feel like being made to take on your brother as an apprentice Septimus."

"Father... Father can't know about this!" Daarshan said. "Jarin is—he is everything to him. And to Mother, as well. I thought—"

"You thought it was because of who Jarin is?" Cat said. "You're right—but in your mother's case, I think who your brother is is the one child she had from a love relationship."

Bina swiped her hair back over her shoulder. "I didn't know it could be like that," she said, her eyes big, "but Mistress Drabet and Master Waldan, they don't love each other. I felt it."

"But they both love Jarin," Daarshan said, his voice heavy with sadness.

"I can't excuse your parents, son," Guy said. "They're fools, both of them. And I could understand if you wanted to punish them. But none of this is your brother's doing."

The boy shook his head. "No," he said, "no. Jarin—Jarin has no idea about this—he can't have. He loves Mother and Father. And he loves the people in this town. It—it would crush him."

"And you care about him too much to do that to him," Bina stated.

He gave her a long look, then nodded. "He's my brother," he said, "he's—he's always been fair to me. Even if—if—"

"—if he calls you names?" Bina said. Daarshan's face twitched in a quickly-suppressed wince. "Yes, you're right," she continued, "he doesn't understand it bothers you when he does. If he did, he'd stop. Because he loves you, too. You know that, right?" She gave him a searching glance.

He gave a nod, then looked up at Guy. "Jarin belongs here. He's the seventh son, that's what everyone thinks. And Mother and Father..."

"Your father thinks he is, and it's what makes him important to him," Bina said, "and your mother knows he's not, and that's what makes him important to *her*. And that's also why she's worried about having you around, because she thinks the truth might come out if your gifts are seen. And Coshy the Poet..."

"He's content with the situation as it is," Cat said. "They had an affair twenty years ago, he wrote some poetry about it—names and identifying details withheld—and that's it, as far as he's concerned. At least that's what I'm picking up from him. He didn't say any of this in so many words, but now that I know about it, I recognize some of the poems. And, he's enjoying watching his own cuckoo in Waldan's nest. I think those two have history, and the affair was as much about Coshy getting his own back as being in love with Drabet."

"I think they still like each other, Master Coshy and Mistress Drabet, I mean," Bina said, "but they want Jarin to be who he is, so they don't say anything."

Slowly Daarshan began, "So that's why Mother is—"

"Maaaaah!" came the frantic cry of the goat from up the hill, beyond the quarry. "Maaaaah, maaaaaah!"

"What the—" Cat started.

"That sounds like goat in trouble," Bina said. "Somebody's gotta go check."

"Maaaaah!"

"I'll go," Cory said. "Jamie, you coming?"

"Sure." They clambered up the slope and disappeared into the woods above the quarry.

Cat turned back to Daarshan. "You'd love to show them all up, wouldn't you?" she said.

There was a gleam in the boy's eyes as he mentally played through that scenario. Cat could picture it—the big showdown at Waldan's house, everyone acknowledging Daarshan as the legitimate Septimus... And she could see on his face the exact moment when he, too, arrived at the next image in the scene, the one where his father was shocked and angry, his mother humiliated, his brother heartbroken and confused as his whole life was shattered...

Daarshan shook his head. "I—I can't. I can't tell everyone. It wouldn't be right."

Guy gave him a nod of approval. "Wise choice," he said. "I knew you were a good man."

Daarshan blinked at the compliment. Then a frown gathered on his forehead again. "But I don't know what—what else..."

"Come back with us, of course!" Bina said, as if it was the most natural thing in the world.

"Yes," said Guy. "Of course."

"But—" Daarshan turned his face up at Guy. "You said you didn't want an apprentice!"

Guy laughed. "I said I didn't want to have your brother as an apprentice Septimus. I didn't say anything about *you*."

Daarshan's face flushed up, and his eyes widened. "I—but—"

"And I can't apprentice you as Septimus," Guy continued, "you have to learn that on your own. I can tell you how it works for me, but I can't teach you how to use your own gift. However, I really do need an apprentice potter. What do you say, son?"

The frantic bleating of the goat had stopped a few moments ago, and suddenly there came a shout from up the hill.

"*Eureka!!*" yelled Jamie.

"Papa, Mumma, Daar!" Cory shouted, "come up here quick! We found blue rocks!"

CHAPTER 27

AT AND GUY WERE walking hand in hand, a good
twenty yards behind the cart. They had crested
the brow of the last major incline before Ruph a little
while ago, and now that the road was level again, all
the kids, plus Eureka the Goat, were riding. Jamie and
Daarshan had had a tussle about who got to drive,
which Daarshan won via "Rock, Paper, Scissors". He
seemed quite proud of himself for his handling of the
reins, judging by the grin he had on his face when Cat
and Guy let the cart get ahead of them.

Cat drew a deep breath of the clean forest air.

"I'm going to miss the ocean," she said, "but boy, am
I glad to be getting home!"

"Are you?" Guy gave her a searching glance.

"Yes, of course! And not only because of seeing the
kids again, either."

"Really? I thought—"

She gave him a look. "What *are* you on about?"

"Didn't you want to—even a little bit—stay there?
The ocean, and fish rolls, and Coshy the Poet..."

Cat snorted. "Yes, and Drabet and Waldan Silver-smith. Being around that family for any length of time would drive me bonkers. Stay there? You've got to be kidding me. I'm glad we went, but..."

He shifted his hand, lacing his fingers through hers. "Then I'm glad too."

She bumped her arm against his. "Besides, I don't think I'd like the potter in that town."

He stopped and pulled her around to face him.

"What exactly do you mean by that, hmm?"

Cat snaked her arms around his neck. "We have much better potters in Ruph," she said, "much superior to potters anywhere else in this world..." She tried to draw his head down for a kiss, but he resisted.

"What about *other* worlds?" he said quietly, looking down at her with a hard-to-read expression in his eyes. "What about—yours?"

"I don't think I know any potters there," she quipped, but then she stopped short. Fear—the look in his eyes was fear. Silly man.

She drew back a little and looked up at him. "Guy. That world is not 'mine' any longer. It hasn't been for ten years. My world is here, where you are."

"So you never wanted to—"

"Leave?" She shook her head. "No. I confess, I get tired of doing everything the hard way all the time—sometimes electricity would sure be nice to have. But—"

He looked away from her. "I'm sorry," he said. "I'm sorry I took you away from all that..."

"You didn't," Cat said. "It was *my* choice to leave that world; my choice to stay here. I don't mind putting up with the lack of mod cons, so long as I have you. And—and that's what's been hard, not having you around much. You've been so busy... But," she repeated, "I can put up with all kinds of stuff, so long as I have *you...*"

He drew a shuddering breath. "Please," he said softly, "please don't *ever* change your mind on that." There was a vulnerability in his look that Cat had not seen in a long time, a sheen of tears covering his turquoise eyes. She pulled his head down, and this time he let her. It was a long, slow, soft kiss that wreaked havoc with Cat's heartbeat, and when they broke apart, there was quite a different sort of gleam in Guy's eyes. He drew her off the road into the thicket, and his hands tightened around her waist.

"So don't you ever forget, Catriona Potterswife,"—his voice was a low, suggestive growl—"that you belong to me!"

Cat twisted out of his grasp, grabbed him by the upper arms, spun him around, and backed him up against a thick tree trunk.

"Oh no, Dyniselm Bookwomansman," she whispered, "you've got it all backwards: it's *you* who belongs to *me*!" She crushed her mouth down on his in a hard kiss. His breathing became laboured, his hands roamed over her back, his fingers tangled in her hair...

"Papa!!" Cory yelled.

Guy groaned. "No! Do they have a sixth sense?"

Cat caught her breath and tried to smooth down her hair. With some reluctance, they stepped back out onto the road. "What is it?"

"Bina says we need to go this way!" Cory pointed down a side path that branched off the road. "But Ruph is that way, I'm sure of it! We all think so, me and Daar and Jamie!"

"It is," Guy said. "That path meets up with the Ilim Road on the other side of town."

"See?" Cory triumphantly turned to his sister.

Bina had a stubborn look on her face. "But we need to go that way!" she said. "I know we do!"

Cat could feel that the girl was upset. She stepped over to her, stroked her hair and tucked a strand behind her ear.

"What is it, sweetie? Why do we need to go that way?"

"I don't know," she said, looking up at Cat with her big turquoise eyes, so much like her father's. Her bottom lip trembled. "There's something we need to do! It's—it's really, really important."

Cory rolled his eyes. "You always say that," he complained. "And besides, that path is too narrow for the cart. I don't want to go that way, I want to go home!"

"Hush," said Cat. "We all want to get home. Bina, does everyone need to go?"

The girl tipped her head and twisted her mouth sideways for a few seconds, then she shook her head. "Nope, not everyone. But *I* do. And—"

"All right, then I'm coming with you," Cat said. "And Guy, you and the boys head home; we'll catch you up. Does that work, Bina?"

The girl vigorously nodded her head.

"I'll go with you," Daarshan said suddenly. He handed the horse's reins to Cory and climbed down from the driver's seat.

They looked at him, surprised.

He blushed a bit. "You might—might need help," he said, "or carry stuff, or—or something."

Guy gave him a nod. "Well done. So—"

Jamie vaulted over the side rail of the cart, landing on his feet on the forest road. "I might as well come too," he said. "My butt hurts from that seat."

Guy smiled his lopsided smile at them. "So you'll be well escorted then, ladies," he said. He climbed up on the cart and pulled Yaya onto his lap. "Let's go, Cory."

"Have you taken this road before, sweetie?" Cat asked Bina as they set out down the narrow forest path.

"I don't think so," the girl replied. "Or maybe once with Aunt, but I don't remember much about it."

They'd carried on in single file for about fifteen minutes, when Bina stopped. She tipped her head to the side, then quickly raised it as if she had heard a sound. She stood perfectly still for a second, as if she was listening, then with a toss of her red hair and a whirl of skirts she hurried down the path.

"Come on," she cried, "we're nearly there! And I know what it is now!" She threw a glance back over her shoulder at Cat. "It's Kashinka!"

"What?" Cat broke into a run to keep up with the girl. "Do you mean she's come back?"

"No," Bina said, not slowing down any, "she hasn't, but there's something she left behind! And I think I know... Come *on*!"

Through the thinning trees, a cottage came into view, a rough little building made of wood planks. In the middle of the clearing in front of it was a large round space where the earth was blackened, charred as if from a series of big bonfires. The charcoal burner's place!

"Who is this we're after?" Daarshan said from behind Cat.

"The chick that ran off with my bowl!" Jamie sounded upset. "The fat grumpy one, who was on the wagon with us when we came here—remember, she got off before we got to town. And then she came and stole my bowl."

"Oh, that was her?" Daarshan said. "She wasn't fat, she was expecting. Actually, if this path is meeting the road to Ilim, maybe this is where she went."

Cat stopped in her tracks and looked around at the boy.

"Kashinka was *what*? And how do you know?"

He shrugged. "I've got sisters."

And then Cat heard the sound of a baby crying.

Bina was flat-out running now.

"Radyam," she called, "Radyam Black!"

She barely stopped to knock on the rough plank door of the cottage, then yanked it open and darted in. The baby's crying stopped.

"Bina!" Cat called, "you can't just—"

She ran after her and peered through the open door into the cottage.

By the empty table in the middle of the room stood Radyam Black, the charcoal burner. She was stuffing an item of clothing into a black-streaked canvas sack and hurriedly tying the bag shut, while her little girl peeked at Cat around her skirts.

"Ah, Catriona Bookwoman," Radyam said. "It's a relief you've come. I was at a loss at what to do with the babe—I must go this instant, or I miss our lift to meet the husband."

"You're moving on then?"

"Yes, he's found us another worksite out Urbron way. I had meant to take the babe to Ouska Wisewoman, but Kelett Carter will go without me if I'm not there shortly." She picked up the little girl, settled her on her hip, and swung her luggage sack by its strap over her shoulder, moving towards the door as if she was leaving.

Cat gave her head a little shake. "Wait—what? This is your little one, isn't she?"

"Yes, that's my little Myra," Radyam said.

"You're not taking her with you?"

Radyam gave Cat a strange look. "Of course I'm taking her," she said. "Say goodbye to Mistress Catriona, sweet." The toddler put her thumb in her mouth and stared at Cat. "Tell Ouska Wisewoman I'm sorry I can't look out for the babe any longer, but Kashinka Proudneck never came back. I only put her up because I owed her a favour, and, well, us women need to help each other out at a time like this. She can look down her nose at me all she wants, but when it comes to birthing, we're all the same."

And then Bina ducked out from the small, narrow doorway at the back of the room, and Cat began to see the light. The girl was cradling a little bundle in her arms, a bundle that, right at that moment, began wailing again—the high, brittle cry of a newborn.

"This is Kashinka's child?" Cat said.

"Yes, of course," Radyam said. "You've come from Ouska Wisewoman for it, have you not?"

Cat shook her head. "Ouska knows about this?"

"No," Bina said, "no, she doesn't. She told me the milk was for your little girl, Mistress Radyam."

"Well, so it was," Radyam said, "at first. But my Myra got better, and I told Kashinka to let Ouska Wisewoman know we had no more need of it. Then Kashinka never came back, and the boy Ouska sent with the milk kept bringing it, so surely Ouska Wisewoman meant it for the babe."

"No," Bina said again, "she didn't know about the baby. Nobody did. Except me, I should have paid attention." She ducked her head, bending over the child she was jiggling in her arms.

"No matter," Radyam said, hitching her little girl higher on her hip. "You've got the babe now. I must go."

"Wait," said Cat. "Let me get this straight. Kashinka came here, to you, to have her baby? Why?"

"As I said, I owed her from when we were children in town, when my mother was her mother's laundrywoman. She came back to Ruph to fetch a thing that belonged to her, she said, but she didn't want to be seen in town in her condition." A flash of contempt ran through Radyam's dark eyes. "Kashinka Proudneck had no wish to have it known in Ruph that she got with child and has no man to show for it."

Cat nodded—that sounded very much like Kashinka.

"But I paid her back what I owed and more, helping her through her time, and I have no more time to nurse her babe," Radyam said. "She can pick up her little bastard from Ouska Wisewoman's, or yours. It's a sweet little thing, in spite of its mother, but I've got my own to look out for. Farewell, Catriona Bookwoman, and give my regards to Ouska Wisewoman." She walked out the door.

For a moment, Cat just stood there, staring at the empty doorframe. And then the thin cries of the child pierced her consciousness, took hold of her and pulled at her heart, drawing her across the room.

She reached out, took the baby out of Bina's arms, and held him close. The moment the child felt her arms around him, he quietened. Cat looked down into the dark brown eyes that gazed up at her solemnly, fastening on her face, and her heart melted.

The baby gave a little hiccough. Then he drew a breath, his face scrunched up, and another wail pierced the air of the cottage.

"He's hungry," Bina said, "he needs milk."

Cat stuck the end of her little finger into the baby's mouth, and he frantically began to suckle.

"I haven't got any milk any more," Cat said, her heart breaking for this little bundle of humanity, unwanted, unloved, abandoned. "It dried up when Yaya weaned himself."

But Bina gave her a wide, brilliant smile, her eyes shining.

"Not you, Mumma—Liss!"

CHAPTER 28

*D*EAR *ANDY, IT'S A boy after all! We were right, Ben and Liss's baby is a boy! We found him at Radyam's house in the forest, me and Mum and Daar and Jamie, where Kashinka left him. He was crying, he was so hungry and sad and wanting a Mumma so much. I felt him, Andy, all his little baby feelings, and it made me cry too.*

We took him to Liss and Ben's, and we ran all the way there. Liss was in the kitchen, cooking Ben's supper, and she'd been crying again, her eyes were all red. I said, "Kashinka birthed him, and she's gone away to Outland and she's never coming back, and he's hungry," and I held out the baby, and he cried so loud. And Andy, she snatched him out of my hands, and she wrapped her arms around him and held him close and looked and looked at him, and then she opened her blouse and put him to her breast to drink, and he sucked and sucked and she cried and cried, so his head got all wet from her tears. But her eyes were shining, and she was smiling so hard, Mum said they were rainbow tears.

And then Ben was there too, and he put his arms around them both and put his head against Liss's, and the baby got even wetter with more tears. Mum says if that wasn't a baptism, she's never seen one before. It's what they do in her old world, they pour water on a baby's head to make him belong and give him a name. And that's what they did, Liss and Ben, they named him right there. They called him Che'anth, like your father, and his eyes are brown like yours and Ben's, and he's got a dimple in his chin ~~that he got from~~ like Liss. (There, I did it again, I already keep forgetting that Liss and Ben aren't his born mother and father. Because he belongs to them, that's why.) He drank all of the milk Liss had right then, and he felt so warm and safe and snug, and then he fell asleep.

Andy, if I hadn't blocked out what I was feeling about Kashinka, I would have known about him, and he could have been home with Liss and Ben that whole time we were in Arkaroth. I did actually know about him, I could feel him, because he's my cousin, but because he's only a baby I didn't know what it was I felt, and I blocked it. It's really no better than what Daar was doing, breaking things because he didn't want to feel his feelings. Mum says it's okay now, it all worked out, and Baby Che is safe and I shouldn't beat myself up over it. But from now on I'm going to pay more attention. I'm going to pay attention to <u>what</u> I'm feeling, not just how much and who from. Mum says I can learn to ~~diffa diffa differench~~ sort out which feelings are important and I need to listen to, and which ones aren't. And I hope I can do that. I knew that what I was feeling about Kashinka <u>mattered</u>, because it was Baby Che.

On the way home from Liss and Ben and Baby Che's, Mum and I stopped at the Garden of Peace. We lit Baby

Daisy's lantern, and it shone out so white and beautiful. I told her that she has a brother, and that her mumma isn't crying for sadness any longer, and then we sang her a lullaby.

And then we went home, and oh Andy, it's good to be home.

Lots of love, Bina

PS: Fionn has finished laying all of the floors for the upper story of the house, and already got the outside walls half done. And Andy, I'm going to get my own bedroom! Mum said her and Papa made some new plans, and the upstairs is going to be made into three rooms, not just one. There'll be one big bedroom for the boys, one for Mum and Papa, _and one for me_! Mine is going to be really small, but I don't care. Love, Bee

CHAPTER 29

JAMIE TOOK ANOTHER CHUNK of bread from the basket in the middle of the table and dunked it into the last bit of the soup in the bottom of his bowl. The soup looked weird, thick and a brownish green, but it sure tasted good—creamy and tangy at the same time. Apparently it was made with sorrel, some sour leafy stuff Cat had growing in the garden beside the house. She said it was a French thing, or at least it was at home. Well, she hadn't said 'at home'—she'd said 'in my old world'. And somehow that made Guy really happy, judging by the look he gave her and the way she smiled back at him. Those guys were embarrassing with how lovey-dovey they'd been acting ever since that trip.

Both of them had gone from the table; Cat to the bedroom next door to put the little guy down for his nap, and Guy to check the kiln, or so he said. For some reason, he'd gone out through the bedroom door to do so. Sure, there was an outside door from that room, but...

However, the next minute he stuck his head back in through the front door. "Kiln is looking good, boys," he said. "We should be able to open it tomorrow."

That was great! Jamie's stomach gave a little twitch of excitement. Only one more day, and he'd get to go home! If—*if* that new glaze worked. He crossed his fingers under the table. Actually crossed them. Because, in a world that he'd ended up in because of making a wish with a little nursery rhyme on a star in a stone, that might make a difference. Or not—but it couldn't hurt, regardless. Go home, finally!

He'd miss these guys here, all of them. Daar, the Ginny kid, all the Weasleys—heck, he'd even miss the stupid goat. If it hadn't been for the animal getting its horns stuck in the bushes above the quarry, they'd never have found the blue stones for his glaze. So he quite liked the goat now.

He wiped the last drops of the soup out of his bowl with the piece of bread and gobbled it down. "Well, that was tasty!" he said, leaning back against the wall and giving a satisfied burp.

"Excuse *you*!" said the kid. "Don't they teach you manners in Outland?"

Jamie grinned at her and burped again, just to bug her.

She wrinkled her nose and crossed her eyes at him, then reached out for the bread basket. So did Cory, at exactly that moment, and their hands closed on the same piece of bread—the last one.

"Hey, I want that!" Cory said.

"So do I!" said Bina. "Why should I let you have it?"

"'Cause... 'cause I'm younger, and I'm still growing!"

"Pfft!" she said. "Then you should let me have it because I'm older and larger and need more food to sus-sustain me."

"If you're going to go with that, it's mine by rights," said Jamie, "I'm the oldest here. But," he waved his hand magnanimously, "you may share it between you, my children. Unless Daar wants it, of course, he's next oldest."

Daar had his chin propped on his hands and was watching their squabble. He shook his head. "I'm full," he said. But he took the bread anyway, tore it in half, then held the pieces out to the kids.

"Very wise," Jamie intoned. "Behold, the wisdom of great age."

Cory tore a chunk off the bread with his teeth. "How old are you actually, Daar?" he said with his mouth full.

"*Akshully*!" Bina mimicked her brother. "You're sixteen, right, Daar?"

Daar nodded.

"When's your birthday?" She took a bite from her bread.

He shrugged. "May 16th."

The kid sprayed breadcrumbs over the table. "What?!? That's today!"

"Oh! Yes, I suppose so." Daar looked surprised, like he hadn't really thought about it.

Bina jumped up from her seat. "Mum!" She bounced over to the bedroom door, but it already opened on its own and Cat came back into the room. "Mum, it's Daar's birthday today! And he didn't tell anybody about it!"

"Oh, is it? Well, happy birthday!"

"Uh, thank you," Daar said, sounding a bit startled.

Bina pulled on Cat's sleeve. "But Mum, we've gotta. .." She stood on tiptoe and whispered in Cat's ear, then said aloud, "Do you think there's enough time?"

Cat smiled at her. "I think so, if we get started right away."

"Oh goody! I'll make the icing!" The kid clapped her hand over her mouth and made big eyes at Daar, afraid she'd given away the secret. She tried a distraction. "So why didn't you tell us?"

"I don't know," Daar said, "I just didn't think of it. My—my family never..."

"Don't you celebrate birthdays?" Bina said.

Daar didn't say anything.

"Hmm." Cat gave Daar a thoughtful look. "Out of curiosity, when is your brother's birthday?"

"Jarin's?" He shrugged again, awkwardly. "The day before yesterday."

Bina was still incensed two hours later, when Jamie walked through town with her on their way back from shopping.

"I can't believe they did that," she said for the umpteenth time. "That stinks, that Daar only ever got birthday leftovers from Jarin! They throw a big party for his brother, and he only gets the leavings! And he didn't even think anything of it, because that's the way it always was. I'm really glad he came to live with us!"

"Yeah, I bet he is too," Jamie said. He was lugging a basket with groceries they had been sent out for, including a little clay bottle of whipping cream for the cake, and a couple of bags of candy. For those, they'd taken a guess at what Daar might like. Bina voted for her own favourite, honey drops, and then they got something that looked like chocolate fudge, plus some dried apricots stuffed with almond paste. They almost got honey-coated hazelnuts, but Jamie remembered just in time that Daar had said he didn't like nuts.

He gestured at the bundle Bina was carrying.

"So do you have wrapping paper or something at home?"

"You mean, to wrap the presents in coloured paper?" she said. "No, we don't do that. Mum said that's what you do in Outland, but we don't. We have a special basket the gifts go in that the birthday person gets to open. Do you think Daar is going to like the shirt we picked out?"

"Probably," Jamie said. "It's pretty nice."

They'd got a brown shirt with some embroidery around the edges from the tailor—the guy who'd played the big kettle drum at the May Day Dance—and then they'd popped by Ben and Liss's and Bina had picked up a sort of wooden pin with a carved head; apparently it was for holding the shirt collar closed, like a stud. Ben had made it; the guy did some seriously fancy wood carving. Bina had spent at least half an hour—okay, maybe fifteen minutes—cooing over the baby, and she insisted that he already looked bigger than when they'd found him a week ago. He certainly looked happier—well, he wasn't squawking any more. And Ben and Liss were totally ga-ga over him.

Jamie couldn't see the appeal of babies himself, but Bina had told him about them losing a kid a little while ago, which sucked pretty bad, so there was a good reason they were happy with this little guy. Ben had a permanent grin on his *Slumdog Millionaire* face now. Jamie was glad things had worked out so well for them all. What a crappy thing to do for that Kashinka chick to just dump her baby! Even if you weren't a baby kind of person, that was plain old wrong. Good thing the kid had found a home. Because home—Jamie mentally struck a sentimental pose to make fun of himself for being so sappy—home was where the heart was.

"So, we got Daar the shirt from Mum and Papa," Bina said, "and the pin, that's from me, and the fudge is from Cory. And Mum is making a cake, and we're having chicken on flatbreads with greens—yum. This'll be great!" She was just about skipping, she was so excited.

"I wish I could have got him something, too," said Jamie, "but I don't have any cash here."

"That's okay," said Bina, "we didn't know ahead of time, else maybe you could have made a present for him. Like—"

"Hey, wait!" Jamie said. "I know!"

Daar kept folding the little scissors out of the Swiss Army knife and putting them back in, a big grin on his face. "For

Frodo," the paper tag said that Jamie had tied to the little ring that was meant for hooking a chain to.

He'd tucked the knife in the birthday basket with the other stuff, and Daar's eyes got bigger and bigger with each thing he took out of the woven wicker container. When he'd got to the knife, Jamie almost thought he was going to cry, and he'd wondered for a second if he'd really stepped on Daar's toes with the 'Frodo' thing. But as it turned out, Daar was just gobsmacked about all the cool presents that he totally hadn't expected.

And then Cat brought out the cake, with the lit candles on top, and Daar looked even more flabbergasted.

Bina clapped her hands with excitement. "This is a special birthday thing we do," she said, "Mum taught us that, from Outland! We sing the birthday song, and then you have to blow out the candles and make a wish."

So they sang "Happy Birthday", and Daar still had this shocked look on his face.

"Blow out the candles!" the little boys cried.

"And you have to wish while you do it!" Cory added.

Daar drew a deep breath. "I wish—"

"Don't say it out loud!" Jamie put in quickly.

"Oh, it won't come true then, right?" Bina said. "Okay, one more time!" She started the last line of the song, and they all chimed in: "Happy Birthday to yoooou!"

Daar huffed out the candles, and they all cheered and clapped.

"And now you've got to cut the cake, so we can all have a piece," Bina declared.

"Cake, cake, cake!" the little boys hollered, bouncing up and down like rubber balls.

Cat handed Daar the big knife to cut the cake with. His eyes were huge, really blue again, and he gripped the knife handle so hard his knuckles were white.

Bina grabbed his wrist and whipped the knife back out of his hand.

"Whoa," she said, "you can't break that!" She laughed up at him. "Don't let your feelings go into the knife."

Guy stepped behind Daar and put his hands on his shoulders. "Yes, please don't ruin my wife's best kitchen knife," he said with a laugh in his voice. "You want to try that one more time, son?"

Bina held the knife out to Daar again, grinning at him.

He looked around at them, still with that semi-shocked look on his face.

"Cake, cake, cake!" All of a sudden little Yaya pinged too far over and collided with his brother; they bounced off each other just like in a cartoon and both landed on their butts on the floor.

There was a stunned silence for a second, then everyone burst out laughing, the little guys shrieking like hyenas.

A smile started to form on Daar's face and got wider and wider. He held out his hand for the knife.

CHAPTER 30

"YOU SHOULD HAVE DONE the Chicken Dance for Cousin Daar's birthday!" Lahni said. "Right, Cousin Jamie?" She tucked her thumbs into her armpits and flapped her elbows. "Cousin Jamie showed us how to do the Chicken Dance at the May Day Dance, Cousin Cat!"

"You did *what*?!?" Cat clapped her hands to her cheeks, staring at Jamie in a fake look of shock. "How could you? The Chicken Dance was the one thing I thought I had safely out of my life forever! And now you had to bring it here?"

Jamie grinned and pointed at Lahni. "It was her fault, she made me do it."

Lahni giggled. "We had fun at the May Day Dance, Cousin Cat," she said. "I'm really good at doing the Chicken Dance!" She wiggled her butt and clapped her hands, humming the tune.

"No, no, spare me!" Cat wailed theatrically, pressing her hands to the sides of her head.

The little boys squealed with giggles. "Show us, Lahni, show us!"

Cat shooed them out into the yard.

"You had some fun here after all, didn't you?" she said with a smile at Jamie, who hung back in the kitchen.

"Yeah," he said, leaning back against the table. "Some of it was a hoot. And that dance... Lahni is—well, she's a sweetie. And nobody seems to think anything of her for being—for—well, you know."

"For being what we'd call 'mentally challenged'? Let alone giving it labels like 'Down's Syndrome', or thinking she can't be a useful member of the community. I know. It's one of the things I love about this place. It's a great place to live."

"Yeah, it's cool," he said. "Still..."

"You're looking forward to going home."

Jamie nodded. "I'm not sure what I'm going to do when I get back, though."

"I'd hope the first thing you'd do is call your parents," Cat said, raising her eyebrows in a Mary Poppins look.

Jamie looked down at the tips of his running shoes, which were looking pretty tattered. They weren't designed for all the walking he'd been doing in the last few weeks. "I don't know," he said, pushing his right toe against the gap that was starting to form between the shoe and the sole. "I've been gone for almost a month. My mom is going to kill me."

"Well, yes! So would I if one of my kids pulled a stunt like that!" Cat folded her arms over her chest. "They've probably been worried sick. But you do know it's because they care about you, right?"

He gave her a look. He wasn't stupid. Of course he knew that about his parents—didn't he?

She smiled back at him. "Just making sure," she said. "But I can see where it would be a bit tricky to explain where you've been. Do you think they'd believe you about all of this?"

Jamie swiped his hair out of his eyes. Amongst other things, he'd have to get himself a haircut as soon as possible. "No," he said. "I'm not sure what I'll tell them. I'll probably think of something."

"I'm sure you will," Cat said. "You're definitely not short on imagination. I'll never forget your rendition of *Harry Potter*; you had the kids spellbound—and the rest of us, too, for that matter. I hope you'll do something with that in the future. Have you thought of going to college?"

Jamie shrugged. "My dad wants me to go," he said, "but I have no idea what I'd take."

"I would have thought that's obvious," said Cat.

He gave her a questioning look.

"Film studies, Neo!" She laughed. "If ever there was a natural for that field, it's you!"

Film studies?

Jamie's surprise must have shown on his face.

"You've never heard of that?" Cat said. "It's like taking English, only you study movies instead of books. Most bigger universities have at least some courses in that. And art schools run courses in film making, of course. You'd be great at that."

Jamie scratched his head. He'd had no idea.

Cat looked over his shoulder through the window out into the yard.

"Oh, good grief," she said, "there's the goat again! At this rate, we might as well keep the critter!"

Bina burst through the door on that last sentence, trailed by one of her little brothers.

"Mum, can we?" she cried.

"Can we what?"

"Keep Eureka! Dyllie thinks she wants to stay with us, right, Dyllie?"

The little boy vigorously nodded his head. "Yup," he said. "Dat's why she's always visitin'."

Cat opened her mouth to answer, but Bina forestalled her.

"We could get Aunt Nicky a new goat," she said. "Please, Mum?"

"Me an' Bina is gonna look after her," Dyllie said.

"And we'll learn to milk her!" the girl added.

Cat shrugged and gave a resigned sigh. "I suppose we could use the milk. And seeing as you've named her, and she travelled all the way to Arkaroth and back with us..."

"...and she found my rocks," Jamie said, "don't forget that."

Bina gave him a bright smile. "Yes, see, Mum? She's done us a service. We *have* to keep her."

"I don't know about 'have to'," Cat said, "but let's say I'll consider it. As long as she doesn't—Oy!!" She rushed out the door into the yard. "Keep that goat away from my garden!"

Dyllie ran out after her, and Bina made to follow. But at the door, she turned around.

"Oh, Jamie, Papa started opening the kiln! That's what I came in here to tell you!"

— *ele* —

There it sat, right in the middle of the big table, all by itself. It was a perfectly proportioned little bowl, quite plain, but it seemed to Jamie that that very simplicity was what made it so extraordinary. The glaze was sparkling blue in the sunshine that fell through the workshop window, an iridescent turquoise or sapphire blue, depending on which angle you looked at it from.

Jamie found that his hands were shaking. Would this really work?

"Yup, it will," Bina said. "It'll take you home."

"It's a pretty bowl, Cousin Jamie," said Lahni.

"Pitty," repeated little Yaya, who could just barely see over the top of the table. He tried to reach for the bowl.

"Don't touch, sweetie," Cat said, catching his hand. "Jamie needs it." She reached out for the bowl to pick it up.

Guy sucked in his breath with a sharp hiss.

Jamie looked up at him, then over to Cat. She had her gaze locked with her husband's. There was a slight smile on her face, like there was some funny secret she had. Very deliberately, never breaking eye contact with Guy, she lowered her hand to the bowl, closed her fingers on it, lifted it up, and moved it a few inches over, out of Yaya's reach, setting it down in front of Jamie with a little thump.

Guy blew out his breath, and his mouth twisted sideways in a smile that looked just a little sheepish. He turned his head and looked at Jamie.

"We'll miss you, son," he said, putting his hand on Jamie's shoulder. "Take care of yourself over there in Outland."

Wow. Jamie ran his hand through his hair. He rated a 'son' from Guy? That was—that was pretty awesome. "Uh, thanks!" he stuttered.

"I wish you didn't have to go!" Bina was beside him, throwing her arms around him.

Lahni got her short arms around him from the other side. "Bye, Cousin Jamie! I'm going to miss you!"

Jamie hugged them both back. Then he hugged the little kids, and even Cory, who looked embarrassed because he was sniffling just a bit. Johnny the Cat came over, too, to rub-hop against Jamie's ankle, and Jamie bent down to scratch him behind the ears. "Bye, kitty," he said, "keep that goat in line, will ya?"

Then Daar held out his hand.

"Farewell, Jamie," he said, "and thank you again for the knife."

"Hey, no problem, man." Jamie gripped Daar's hand and thumped him on the upper arm with the other. Daar slapped him back, and all of a sudden they were having one of those guy tussles that said "I don't want to hug you because that would be way too mushy but you're pretty cool anyway," and then they were both clearing their throats and trying not to look at anyone in particular.

"My turn," Cat said, and she gave Jamie a hug too. "Say hi to 'Outland' for me."

"Uh, thanks again for everything," he stammered, "and..."

"You're very welcome," Cat said, "It was great having you. And now I think you'd better get going."

"So, uh, how does this work?" Jamie said. He looked at the bowl which was twinkling at him with little star-like pinpricks, daring him to touch it.

"You make a wish, and you pick it up," Bina said, "right, Mum?"

"Yes," Cat said. "Do it, Jamie."

Jamie drew a deep breath and looked around the circle. "Okay, here goes nothing." He reached out for the bowl, and then, just because, he broke into the chant.

"Star light, star bright..."

The kids joined in the rhyme, and they all sang together,

"The first star I see tonight,

"I wish I may, I wish I might

"Have the wish I wish tonight!"

Jamie's fingers closed on the bowl.

"I wish..."

"*Don't say it out loud*!" the kids cried, but a blue, sparkly maelstrom surged up around Jamie, spinning, circling—and he was whirled away in its light, all sense of place lost.

CHAPTER 31

J AMIE STAGGERED, LOST HIS balance and hit the
ground with a thump. The bowl flew out of his hands.
"Whoa!" he cried out, expecting to hear the sound of
crashing pottery, but none came.

The blue whirling light around him slowed down and
then floated away, the way the stars you see after you've hit
your head gradually disappear from your vision. Jamie's
surroundings slowly came into focus.

In the dull light of an overcast day, a blue-grey rock wall
rose in front of him, completely filling his field of vision.
At the same time, he became aware that his right hand,
pressed to the ground where he had broken his fall, had
sharp rocks digging into it.

Rocks!

Rock wall!

No—not the quarry again!

He frantically whipped his head to the left—another
rock wall! Then to the right—there too! No, it couldn't
be! Not again! Not—

But wait.

These weren't the rough walls of a quarry. They were perfectly smooth, perfectly straight. They met at right angles in the corner. They had—Jamie tipped his head back and let his gaze travel upwards—they had *windows* in them, for crying out loud!

Jamie pulled himself together, and he looked around himself properly this time. He was in the back courtyard of a U-shaped building, blue-grey stuccoed walls rising in front and on two sides of him, gravel on the ground around him.

He pushed himself up off the ground and turned all the way around.

A grassy park area opened up behind him, dotted with trees.

"Another one, huh?"

The voice came from Jamie's left. He turned, and there against the corner of the building squatted a scruffy-looking guy, one hand buried in the pockets of a dirty brown trenchcoat, the other holding a short stub of a cigarette. The man pointed his stubble-covered chin at something behind Jamie. "But hers broke when she landed. Might even still be some bits around somewhere."

Jamie stared at the guy. "Her what?"

"That dish of yours," the man said. "Same colour as hers, too."

Jamie slewed his head around to where the man was looking. His bowl! There it was, safe and sound, sitting on the ground, its amazing blue glaze contrasting with the dirty gravel. Jamie scooped it up. Not even a nick.

"What do you mean by 'her'?"

The man levered himself up from the ground.

"The chick that landed here a coupla weeks back," he said. "Same thing, a coloured sort of whirlwind, then there she was, landed on her ass. And she had a dish just like this. Except when she dropped hers, it broke." He scuffed the toe of his ratty-looking shoe in the gravel close to the wall. "Ah, there." He bent down, picked something out of the dirt, and held it out to Jamie. "That was a piece o' hers."

Jamie looked closer. It was a pottery shard, the clay a red terracotta colour, what was still visible of the glaze a dull brown tone.

"That's not like mine," he said, "look, totally different colour."

"Like hers before it broke," the guy said around the cigarette stump in the corner of his mouth. "First it was blue like yours, then *bam*, busted and all ugly brown. How much you want for yours?" He stretched his brown hand out for Jamie's bowl.

Jamie pulled it out of the man's reach. "It's not for sale," he said. "What happened to—to the woman?"

The man gave a rough-voiced chuckle. "I watched her throw a hissy fit for a while," he said. "Run out into the park, around the corner, freak out at the cars and run back here again, in and out a coupla times."

Cars? That was right, Jamie hadn't even realized it at first—he could hear the roar of twenty-first century city traffic from beyond the building.

"Uh, where exactly are we?"

"Greenward Falls, they call this place." The man sucked the last bit of smoke out of the cigarette stub, then tossed it to the ground. He tipped his head at the building behind him. "That's the museum there."

"So, uh—Canada? Or the States? Or what?"

"The You-nited States of Aaaah-merika," the man said, drawing out the vowels mockingly. "That mean somethin' to you? Didn't to her."

"No, it wouldn't," said Jamie. "She's from—uh, never mind. So what'd you do with her?"

"Took her to the homeless shelter—eventually," the guy said. "She didn't like it. Looks like she landed on her feet though. Saw her again a coupla days ago, with some real fancy chick—some fashion model or somethin'. Coulda been a sister o' hers, 'cept she's got black hair and the other chick kinda bleach-blonde. Hardly recognized her, all dressed up. And she was pretendin' not to see me. I guess once you're outta trouble, you don't give a shit about the guy that helped you when you were down." He cleared his throat and spat on the ground.

"Yeah," Jamie said. "If that's the same chick I met—I don't see how it could be anyone else—she's a piece of work. So, uh—I don't suppose there's a pay phone around here somewhere?"

A sudden gust of wind whipped around the corner of the building, and the guy turned up the collar of his coat. He shook his head. "Not that I've seen."

"Damn."

Some heavy drops of rain splashed on Jamie, and then it was as if someone had turned on a faucet over their heads.

"This way!" the guy said, and they ran to get out of the deluge, around the building and up a broad set of stairs, ducking into a kind of porch in front of a wide set of doors.

Jamie pulled on the door handle, but it didn't budge.

"Closed today," the man said. "Tuesday."

"Damn," Jamie said again, "just my luck. I was hoping they'd let me use their phone for a collect call."

"Who you tryin' to call?"

"My folks," Jamie said. He turned his back to the rain blowing in under the porch roof. What was he going to do?

The man gave him a look from under his dark eyebrows, a long, assessing stare, as if this piece of information somehow had changed his opinion of Jamie.

"You got family here?"

Jamie nodded, disheartened. "In Canada. Yeah."

The man suddenly dug his hand into his pocket.

"Here," he said. "It's got some minutes left on it. Keep it." He clapped something into Jamie's hand, then abruptly turned and started down the stairs, his head low and his shoulders hunched against the rain.

Jamie stared down at his hand to see a battered old flip phone, its one corner bashed in and the outside screen scratched so badly you could barely see the display. But there *was* a display—it obviously still had power.

"Hey, wait!" He dashed out into the rain after the guy. "You—hang on! Don't you need this?"

The man looked at him over his shoulder. "Found it in the ditch," he said curtly. "I ain't got nobody to call." For a moment he looked at the bowl in Jamie's hand with a weird, hungry expression. "Take it, call your people."

He turned and strode away.

Jamie looked down at the bowl. The raindrops were spattering on its blue glaze, distorting the light. A fat drop landed right in the middle of the bottom and sat there, like a tiny magnifying glass, and for a split second, a small, perfectly clear white star twinkled up at Jamie.

He looked at the cell phone in his other hand.

And ran down the last few steps to catch up with the guy.

"Here," he said, thrusting the bowl at him. "And thank you."

The man's head jerked up and he stared at Jamie, his black eyes wide, showing the little blood-shot veins in the corners.

Then his hands shot out; he grabbed the bowl and clutched it against his chest.

It was almost as if someone had wiped a sponge over the guy's face, his expression changed so completely. In the blink of an eye, he went from a cynical, broken-down bum to—to someone with hope, with a purpose.

"My thanks," he said, his voice sounding half-choked like he had a hard time getting the words out, "my deepest thanks, young master!" He gave a bow, exactly like Daar was always doing. "My obligation is greater than I can summon speech." And he spun on his heel and strode away into the rain, his head held high.

Jamie blinked.

Was it his imagination, or had the guy just turned Shakespearean on him? And where had he seen an expression in someone's eyes like that, very recently, too?

He gave his head a shake, then flipped open the phone.

With shaking fingers, he stabbed out the familiar ten-digit sequence and hit the button with the little green phone symbol on it. One ring. Two rings. Three. He jiggled his knee. Four rings. Fi-

"Hello?"

"Hi, Mom? It's—"

"*JAMIE!!!*"

<hr />

Jamie leaned back into the soft car seat and took a swig from his coke can, enjoying the familiar hum of the Honda's engine. They had just left the border crossing behind; another hour would get them home.

Mom took out a bag and looked back over her shoulder at Jamie. "Do you want a sandwich?"

"Sure! Thanks." He bit into the soft, squishy bread. "Mmm, that's sure different from Cat's sourdough bread."

"This, uh, commune you were staying with," Mom said, "how far away from that Greenward Falls place is it?"

"Mm-mph," Jamie mumbled, pointing at his cheeks stuffed full of peanut butter and jelly to show her he couldn't answer at the moment. Not that he had any intention of doing so when his mouth was empty, either, but there was no need to tell her so.

"Don't pry, Marg," Dad said, putting on the indicator and changing lanes. Jamie still couldn't believe they'd both come to pick him up—and apparently Jessica would have been there too if she hadn't been stuck in an important work meeting when they were leaving to get him. Dad had taken the whole afternoon off work to come.

"I'm not prying, John!" Mom said. "I'm just curious. And Kaden didn't know anything about where Jamie had gone, so, I just want to know. You don't mind, Jamie, right?" She looked back at him with a smile. Actually, he did mind—it was hard to keep his story straight. He hadn't yet had to resort to the "I don't want to talk to you because I'm a grumpy teenager" act, but it probably wouldn't be long.

Dad chuckled. "Even if he did, you'd probably not stop," he said. "Got another PBJ for me, or is it all reserved for the prodigal son?"

Mom passed him a sandwich, too. Dad was in an amazingly good mood. Jamie had been a bit apprehensive when he saw them both climbing out of the car, but as of yet, he hadn't once got that look from Dad, the one he dreaded. Instead, Dad had given him a big hug; between that and what Cat had said, Jamie was actually starting to believe that Dad had been worried about him.

Mom massaged her temples and made a bit of a face.

"Are you okay, Mom?"

She looked back at Jamie with a surprised expression. "Only one of my headaches," she said, "not that big a deal."

Jamie suddenly realized that he'd never really paid attention to how his parents were feeling, never mind asked them about it, and he shook his head at himself. Bina and her feely-clairvoyance must have rubbed off on him.

Mom took a little container out of her purse and shook a couple of pills onto her hand. Small, round, *bright red* pills.

"Mom?" Jamie's voice came out a little squeaky. "What the heck are those?"

"Just some painkillers, over-the-counter stuff," she said, popped the pills into her mouth and took a swig from her water bottle to swallow them down.

Painkillers. Just—some—painkillers. Over-the-counter *painkillers*! And he'd thought... Wow.

"So, the commune," Mom started up again, "where exactly is this place? Which highway? How do you get up there?"

"They're, uh, off the grid out there," Jamie said, "you have to pretty much hike in. No cell reception, either." Which was all honest-to-goodness truth.

"Sounds restful," Dad said.

"That's what Cat says. You miss technology a bit, but it's a much more peaceful life."

"So, this Cat," said Mom, "is she someone special?"

"She's pretty nice, yeah," Jamie said. "Why?"

"Oh, just wondering." Mom flipped down the sun visor and looked at Jamie in the little mirror that was attached to it. "Are we ever going to meet her?"

"Uh, I don't think so. Like I said, off the grid."

"What your mom is trying to ask you," said Dad with a grin, "is whether Cat's your girlfriend."

Jamie spewed a mouthful of pop all over his pants.

"Damn! Uh, sorry, but—NO!"

"Really? Why not?" Mom passed him a handful of paper napkins.

Jamie dabbed at his pants and the back of Mom's seat. "For one, she's way too old—sorry, Mom, I mean, she's not as old as you guys, but, uh, anyway. And besides," he added, "Guy would kill me." He shuddered to think what Guy in a jealous rage would be like—one taste of his temper had been quite enough.

"Who's Guy?"

"Cat's husband. They've got, like, half a dozen kids—wait, no, just five, I think—and they're all redheads. Like the Weasleys."

"The Weasleys? Are they part of the commune, too?"

Dad shot a look at Mom. "No, Marg—they're from *Harry Potter*. Don't you remember when we took the kids to see the movies?"

"Oh! No, I didn't go; you took them by yourself."

That was right—it had been Dad who'd taken Jamie and Jessica to see the first movie, when Jamie was really little. And Dad had picked him up and held him on his lap when he'd freaked out about the scary Voldemort face at the big climax scene, and Jamie had hidden his face on Dad's chest until he wasn't so scared any more and he was able to watch the happy ending with the steam train, which he'd thought was awesome. Jamie remembered it now—how scary it had been, and how being held by Dad had made him feel safe and okay. He'd forgotten about that until just now.

"Uh, Dad?"

Dad looked at him in the rearview mirror. Jamie had never before noticed that they had the exact same eye colour, sort of a greeny-brown. "Yes?"

"You know that money from Grandpa George for college—is it still available?"

CHAPTER 32

"CATRIONA BOOKWOMAN," FIONN CALLED up the stairs, "are you up there?"

Cat walked to the head of the staircase, her arms full of bedding. "Yes?"

"You'll want to come down here and see if the goat pen is to your liking before I get the final nails in," the builder called.

"I'll be right there."

She went back into her new bedroom—a real bedroom with an actual door!—put the blankets on the bed and took a look out the window. The goat pen was looking good, built up against the workshop on the other side of the courtyard. Eureka the Goat, tethered to a tree not far from it, was inspecting the proceedings, while Dyllie was inspecting the goat. Cat smiled—so far the little boy's attentions to the animal had been keeping the goat happy, so she had not seemed to be in need of another four-footed companion. Today she was acting a little more cranky, though—she had been bleating non-stop for the last half hour, and kept pawing the ground. Maybe she was getting antsy for her new home.

Cat went downstairs and out through the kitchen door.

"Mumma!" Dyllie called as soon as Cat set foot into the yard, "Mumma, dere's something yucky coming out of Eureka's bum!"

"Don't touch it," Cat called. "I'm sure she'll be all right, just leave her be."

"But it's really, really yucky! And she's lied down!"

Cat went over to the goat.

"Now she's getting up again!" Dyllie said.

Fionn Builder ducked out of the goat pen.

"Catriona Bookwoman, you'll want to... Ah, what's this then?" He walked across, took a look at the goat and let out a snort. "Looks like you got that pen just in time."

"Do you mean what I think you mean?" Cat said. She looked at the goat. A shiny, sac-like thing bulged out of the animal's rear end.

Fionn had already turned back to the goat shed. "Oh yes," he said over his shoulder, "that goat's kidding all right. I don't know much about it, the wife deals with the animals at our house, but I've seen it happen a time or two. I'll finish this up then, shall I?"

The second window in the new upper story of the house opened, and Bina hung her head out.

"What's going on, Mum?"

"Eureka is pooping out a baby!" Dyllie yelled back gleefully.

"What? Really? Cool!" Bina's red hair whirled around like a flag, her head disappeared from the window, and a few seconds later she came bursting out of the kitchen door. "How long is this going to take? What's going to happen?"

Cat pressed her hands to her cheeks.

"I have no idea," she said. "I didn't even know the goat was pregnant! How could I not know this? How could the goat be pregnant and none of us have a clue?"

"It happens," said Bina wisely. "Aunt says specially with first-time nanny goats it's hard to tell sometimes."

"First-time nannies, and first-time nanny goat owners," Cat said. "So you've discussed goat birthing with Aunt, have you? Well, in that case we should be all set."

Bina ran her hands over the goat's swollen belly.

"We talked about it 'cause I thought Aunt's goat was pregnant, 'cause she had a big fat belly like this too," she said, "and I wanted to see a baby born. But Aunt said not. That's when she said that about nanny goats, that you don't always know." Then she gave Cat a big smile. "It'll be okay, Mum, I can tell."

"Now you can feel goats, too?"

"No, not really—not like people," the girl said. "But I can still tell it'll be okay."

"Wow," said Cat a few hours later, snuggled up to Guy's side, "this has been one eventful month! And now to cap it off we've got twin goats. Too bad Jamie wasn't here any more to see them born." She laughed. "I would have liked to have seen his face at that—a goat birth is gross; I had no idea."

Cat could see Guy's lopsided grin in the moonlight that fell through the bedroom window. "It would have sent him screaming back to Outland, if he hadn't wanted to go already." He shifted the arm that was lying under Cat so he could look down at her. "But it doesn't you?"

Cat pillowed her head on his chest.

"Don't be silly," she said, "I'm made of sterner stuff. And besides, I told you—this is home. I'm not going anywhere. So don't think you can get rid of me that easily."

She poked Guy in the ribs, which led to him having to wrap both arms around her to prevent further assaults.

"I'm going to miss Jamie, though," Cat said a while later. "He's a good guy. I hope things go well for him back in 'Outland'."

"You could always name one of the goats after him, to remember him by," Guy said drowsily. "Or our next baby."

Cat smiled.

"No," she said, "not the baby." She laid a hand over her belly. "He's called Marin."

"What?!?" Guy twisted around in bed and shoved himself up on one elbow, suddenly wide awake. "He *is* called that?"

"That's right." Cat smiled up at him. "Marin means 'of the sea'. I thought we could name him after the place where he got his beginning—don't you agree?"

Guy leaned down and kissed her. "Of course I do, Karana," he said. "Whatever you think is right, that's just what we will do."

NOTE

Names in the Septimus World don't quite work the same way they do in ours.

People have their given names; some are called by those, but many have nicknames which might or might not have anything to do with their real name—such as Guy, whose name is really Dyniselm, and his brother Risyl, who was nicknamed Sepp on the mistaken assumption of his being the Septimissimus. They use their nicknames in everyday life, and reserve their given names for Sunday best, as it were.

Last names, however, are not the same as they are in our world: second names are more like labels, so they can change with the situation. Guy can be called Guy Potter (according to his profession), or Guy Septimus (after his family), or Guy Septimissimus (naming his position). Children can be called after their parents or parents' profession (so Bina might be called Ysbina Potterschild), and spouses after each other (when Cat isn't Catriona Bookwoman or Catriona Outlander, she is occasionally Catriona Potterswife). The name might even describe physical characteristics—Radyam got her label "Black" not only because of her dark hair, but because of the coal dust from her charcoal burner's job.

GLOSSARY

THE PEOPLE OF *STAR BRIGHT*

Cat (Catriona), librarian, mum. Also called Bookwoman or Septimuswife.

Guy (Dyniselm), Cat's husband. Potter, Septimissimus.

Bina (Ysbina, Bibby), Guy's daughter from his first marriage.

Cory (Coryell), Cat and Guy's first son.

Kell (Kelroda), their second son.

Dyllie (Aldyl), their third son

Yaya (Iawar), their fourth son.

Andy (A'verelm), Guy's former apprentice and Bina's confidant. Clay sculptor. Lives in Rhanathon.

Ekinoru, Andy's master.

Ben (Br'oldyn), Andy's twin. Woodcarver.

Nygelis (Liss), his wife.

Lahni (Sulahna), Cat's household assistant.

Dola, her mother

Jamie Coleman, 19. Recently graduated from high school.

Kaden, Jamie's friend.

Hallie, Kaden's sister, owns a shop.

Daarshan, 16. Eighth son, from Arkaroth.

Waldan, Silversmith. Daarshan's father

Drabet, his mother.

Jarin, his seventh brother.

Coshy the Poet, netmaker.

Fionn, builder.

Radyam Black, charcoal burner.

Sepp (Rysil), Guy's brother. Woodworker.

Nicky (Monica), Sepp's wife. Designer, mum.

Uncle (Sardor), Guy's Uncle. Brewer.

Aunt (Ouska), Uncle's wife. Wisewoman.

Chonyk, their son. Farmer.

Rhitha (Rhee), Bina's cousin.

Kashinka, her sister.

Kim (Kimira), Liss' sister.

Kaltas, her boyfriend.

John, Marg and Jessica Coleman, Jamie's parents and sister.

The Goat.

Johnny the Cat. Three-legged, lives with the Septimus family.

Crookshanks the Cat, lives in Hallie's shop.

THE PLACES OF *STAR BRIGHT*

Ruph, the town

Isachang, the country

Ilim, a city on the plains

Arkaroth, a small fishing town

Rhanathon, a large city on the coast

Greenward Falls, an American town where Cat and Nicky came from

ACKNOWLEDGEMENTS

As always, my thanks go to the wonderful people without whom this book would not be what it is:

Peter, Anna, Louise, Kate, and Elke, who alpha-, beta-, and proof-read the first edition.

The members of my Critique Group, who told me they didn't like Jamie the way he was and that they found some of the scenes confusing, which made me give him a cat to pet and clear up his drunken ramblings. He's a better man for it.

A special shout-out goes to Anna, who, when I was complaining about how boring my writing was, said, "Put in a goat!" So I put in a goat.

And because I didn't know much of anything about goats, Kate M. Colby came to the rescue, and her expert advice helped Eureka the Goat become what she is.

Maaaah! I mean, Thank You.

ABOUT THE AUTHOR

A. M. Offenwanger lives in rural Western Canada with her family, which includes two cats, numerous dust bunnies, and a small stuffed bear named Steve. She is happiest when she has her feet in the ocean surf and is quite fond of sushi. Online she can be found on Facebook and Instagram, and on her website, www.amoffenwanger.com.

www.ingramcontent.com/pod-product-compliance
Lightning Source LLC
Chambersburg PA
CBHW031718170626
46808CB00005B/1796